COOPER'S CORNER CHRONICLE

Music Lovers Flock to Twin Oaks

Since its opening last fall, Twin Oaks Bed and Breakfast has continued to attract guests as well as residents of Cooper's Corner to its teatime tradition. The gathering room is the perfect setting for a cup of tea and a sample of Clint Cooper's excellent baking, but many would confess that the main draw is the soul-soothing music provided by Beth Young at the piano.

Beth has lived in Cooper's Corner for the past couple of years, and most days she can be found at her usual post as town librarian. She says it's a privilege for her to play at Twin Oaks, since she has no piano of her own, and she's happy if her music is a source of pleasure for others. Of course, most people agree that Clint Cooper is probably Beth's number one fan. Seems he can't drag himself away from the gathering room when she's playing!

If you haven't yet had the experience, make your way up to the white farmhouse on top of the hill, settle into a cozy chair with a cup of tea or a glass of wine and let the wonder of Beth's music lift all your cares away.

W9-CPB-275

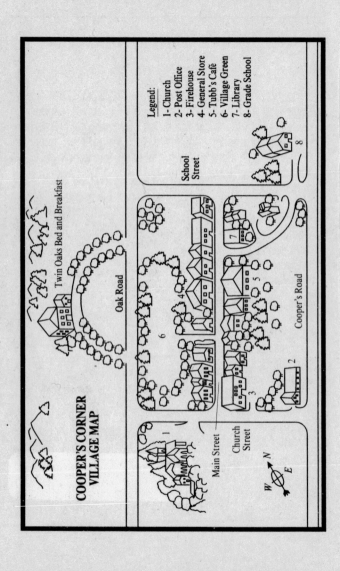

COOPER'S CORNER

AMANDA STEVENS

Her
Stolen Past

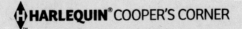

HARLEQUIN® COOPER'S CORNER

ISBN-13: 978-0-373-82662-9

HER STOLEN PAST

Amanda Stevens is acknowledged as the author of this work.

Printed in U.S.A.

⊞ HARLEQUIN®
™ www.Harlequin.com

Dear Reader,

When I first got the call to write this book, I was thrilled to be included in the Cooper family's story, but also a bit intimidated. After all, it would be my job to breathe life into handsome, sophisticated Clint Cooper, co-owner of Twin Oaks Bed and Breakfast. But as I began to dig beneath the surface, I soon realized I was in familiar territory. Clint is just a small-town boy at heart, steadfast, loyal and down-to-earth. He's a widower wounded by a devastating betrayal, and a father intent on protecting his son at any cost.

Enter Beth Young, a woman with a stolen past; a beautiful siren whose music lures Clint into dangerous waters and threatens the peaceful, idyllic life he's created for his family in Cooper's Corner.

I hope you enjoy Clint and Beth's journey and find as many surprises along the way as I did.

Happy reading!

Amanda Stevens

THE COOPERS OF COOPER'S CORNER

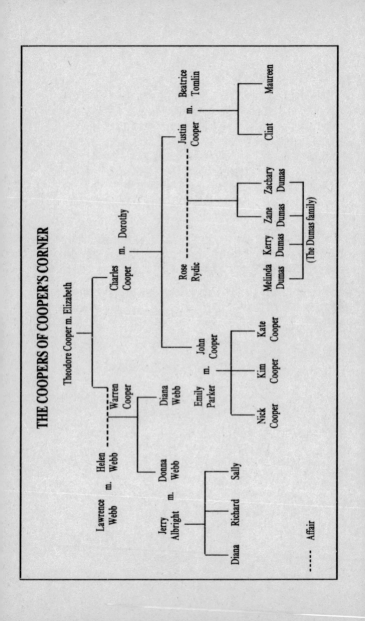

CHAPTER ONE

WHEN SHE AWAKENED, she felt as if she'd been asleep for a very long time, Rip Van Winkle arising from a twenty-year slumber. She had the oddest sensation of having been trapped in suspended animation while the world around her continued to turn. A series of tubes and wires that ran from space-age-looking machines to her bed, to *her,* did nothing to dispel the image.

Something beeped on one of the screens, and panic mushroomed inside her. Where was she? What had happened to her? She couldn't seem to remember.

She tried to bring her surroundings into clearer focus, but the effort was too great. Her eyes fluttered closed, and she could feel herself drifting off to a place that might have been home.

Home...

"Welcome back, honey."

She hadn't even been aware that her eyes were open, but suddenly she saw a face peering down at her.

"Jane? Can you hear me?" the woman in green scrubs asked anxiously.

What's wrong with me? she wanted to know, but the croak that came from her mouth frightened her.

"Take it easy," the nurse said soothingly. "You haven't used your vocal cords in a while so they're bound to be a bit rusty. Plus you had a tube down your throat to help you breathe.''

A tube down her throat? That sounded serious.

The nurse leaned over her. ''Do you know where you are?''

''Hospital…?''

The woman beamed at her. ''That's right. Can you tell me your name?''

She searched her mind. There was nothing inside her head but a thick, gray haze. ''Jane…?''

''That's what we've been calling you because we didn't know your real name. Can you tell me now?''

Her eyes filled with tears as she shook her head.

The nurse patted her arm. ''There, there. It's understandable you're a bit confused after everything you've been through. Are you in pain?''

Her head felt strange, she realized. She tried to lift her hand to the source of the discomfort, but the nurse caught her wrist and brought it back down.

''Just lie still now. I need to let Dr. Wesley know you're awake. You've been drifting in and out on us for a couple of days now. He'll be glad to know you're finally alert. Hang in there, okay? I'll be right back.''

Panic welled inside her again. She tried to catch the nurse's sleeve, but her hand felt so heavy she let it fall helplessly to the bed.

''Where…?''

''You're in San Bernardino County Hospital. You've been in Intensive Care for three weeks. It was touch and go for a while, but you're going to be just fine.''

Three weeks? She'd lost three weeks of her life? "What...happened...?"

"You were in a car accident. You don't remember that, either? Well, don't worry. I'll get the doctor, and he'll explain everything."

After the nurse was gone, Jane lifted her left hand—the right was encased in a heavy cast—to her head, and felt a thick bandage that covered a good portion of her skull. All around the gauze was nothing but smooth skin. Her head had been shaved, and for some reason, that discovery terrified her more than anything else.

DR. WESLEY DIRECTED a penlight at her eyes, checking the dilation of her pupils. "How are you feeling today, Jane?"

"Much stronger." She also felt more alert and focused than she had since she'd awakened from her coma the day before, even though there were aspects of her condition she still found very confusing. "But I can't remember anything. Not even my own name." A note of desperation crept into her voice. "You said temporary amnesia isn't unusual following a head injury, but it almost always goes away. Why isn't mine going away?"

"Every patient is different. I can't give you an exact timetable." Dr. Wesley flicked off the light and slipped it into the pocket of the white lab coat he wore over a faded T-shirt and jeans. He was youngish, no more than thirty-five, but his blue eyes radiated both intelligence and compassion, making her want to trust him. "Maybe it would help you better understand your condition if I fill you in on some of the details of the accident and the injuries you sustained. Are you up for that?"

She nodded, although she wasn't at all certain that she was.

He pulled up a stool and sat down. "The best we can tell, you were traveling alone down Big Bear Mountain. Does that ring any bells?"

She searched her mind. "No."

"There was a heavy rainstorm that night. The roads were very slick. Your car went over the side of the mountain into a deep ravine. According to an eyewitness, the vehicle rolled at least twice. If you hadn't been wearing your shoulder belt, you would probably have been thrown through the windshield."

A horrifying image, made more so by the fact that she had trouble picturing her own face, even though she'd studied her features at length that morning in a hand mirror the nurse had given her.

She couldn't think of herself as Jane, either, but that was what everyone at the hospital called her. Jane Doe was the name they gave unidentified dead women, wasn't it? And contrary to her appearance, she was very much alive.

"At the bottom of the ravine, the car plunged into a river," Dr. Wesley said. "Luckily, the man who saw you go over the mountain called 911 on his cell phone. He had ropes and a flashlight in his truck, and he climbed down the ravine to help you. But by the time he got to the bottom, the currents had swept both you and the car downstream. You must have still been conscious at that point because you were able to free yourself and swim away.

"When the man finally found you, you'd been

washed up against an outcropping of rocks. He didn't know how badly you were hurt or how long you'd been underwater. He didn't even know if you were still alive, but once he got you out of the water, he administered CPR while he waited for the rescue team and the paramedics. He saved your life.''

She fought back sudden tears. It seemed so ungrateful that she had no recall, not even so much as a glimmer of this nameless, faceless hero who had saved her.

''You were suffering from hypothermia,'' Dr. Wesley continued. ''A broken wrist, multiple cuts and contusions, a severe head wound. You may have noticed we had to give you a new haircut.'' When his attempt at humor fell flat, he abandoned any pretense of a bedside manner and became briskly professional once again. ''You lost a lot of blood before the ambulance arrived. You were in shock. On the way to the hospital, you went into cardiac arrest.''

''You mean—''

''Your heart stopped. You had to be resuscitated twice. Once in the ambulance and once in the E.R.''

She'd died and been brought back to life twice. Maybe Jane Doe was an appropriate name, after all.

''You slipped into a coma,'' he said. ''And until you woke up yesterday morning, we had no way of knowing the extent of the damage to your brain.''

She didn't say anything, but he must have seen the terror in her eyes because he hurried to reassure her. ''I know it sounds bad, but any trauma to the head can cause bruising of the cerebral cortex, which is the part of the brain that deals with memory. Amnesia is usually one of the first problems patients experience after a head injury, and it's one of the last of the cognitive functions to return.''

"But it does return. Right?''

"Most of the time.'' He hesitated, as if considering how much more he should tell her. "There's still a lot about amnesia we don't understand, but what we do know is that different types of information are stored in different parts of the brain. What this means is that personal memories can be lost while more general memories are left intact. In other words, you can forget your name but still remember how to talk.''

"That's something to be thankful for, I guess.''

"It's a great deal to be thankful for. I've heard of patients who've had to relearn how to talk, how to walk, how to feed themselves. I think, under the circumstances, you can count yourself lucky.''

She felt ashamed of her self-pity. After what he'd just told her, it was a miracle she was alive.

"But to be honest,'' he said slowly, "I'm a little concerned that your memory loss is as complete as it is. Normally, in retrograde amnesia such as yours, there are isolated events that the patient remembers quite well. Incidents that occurred a few weeks, months or even years prior to the injury. These 'islands of memories' can help trigger other memories. Usually during the healing process, the islands get larger and larger until memory is restored. In some instances, the use of photographs or personal stories from the patient's past can also help, but since your identification was lost in the accident and we don't know how to contact your next of kin, there's nothing much we can do but wait.''

"For how long?''

"As I said, each patient is different. Most memories are recovered within seventy-two hours or so after the injury is first sustained. In your case, the coma may have complicated the process. On the other hand, it also gave your brain time to heal."

She stared up at him anxiously. "What are you trying to tell me, Dr. Wesley?"

He met her gaze. "The fact that you're still unable to retrieve memories three weeks after the trauma occurred could indicate that the damage to your brain is more severe than we anticipated. It's possible you may never get your memory back."

BY THE END OF THE WEEK, Jane was well enough to be moved from the ICU into a semiprivate room on the third floor. The other patient was an elderly woman with dandelion fluff for hair and blue-veined hands that fluttered like restless butterflies against the white sheets. She watched with avid curiosity while the nurse helped Jane settle in.

"I'm Addie," she finally blurted, as if she'd remained silent for as long as she could stand to. Propped up against a stack of pillows, she looked frail and wan, about a hundred years old, but her eyes gleamed with a kind of mischievous vitality that age and illness were hard-pressed to subdue. "I have leukemia and I'm dying, but I'm not saying that to get your sympathy. I just don't want you lying there wondering why I have no eyelashes."

Jane didn't quite know how to respond to such candor. "They call me Jane Doe," she said hesitantly, "because I don't know my real name. I have brain damage, and I've already clinically died twice."

Addie stared at her for a moment, speechless. Then she burst out laughing. "Okay, you win. Brain damage, amnesia, a double flat-liner. That makes leukemia sound downright boring."

Jane hadn't meant to be funny, but Addie's laughter was infectious. She found herself grinning back at the older lady, as if the two of them shared some hilarious, private joke. The nurse paused at the door, gazing back at them and shaking her head, no doubt thinking they were both crazy. Her expression made Addie laugh even harder.

From that moment on, Jane didn't feel quite so alone. It was hard to explain, but she was drawn to Addie from the first, perhaps because they were both facing the unknown. In some ways what lay ahead of Jane seemed a little like death. A dark, one-way journey with no recognizable exits, no U-turns, no going back to the life she'd once had.

It was a frightening prospect, her future, but Addie had a way of helping her find humor in even the most unlikely circumstances. "I like your hair," she'd remarked quite seriously the day Jane's bandages had come off, and she knew Jane was feeling particularly self-conscious about her appearance. "Not everyone can wear a buzz cut, but it looks good on you. Of course," Addie added, smoothing her own cottony tufts, "chemo has done wonders for my glorious tresses."

Another day, when Jane had been brooding about her memory loss and how she would cope once she was out of the hospital, Addie had announced out of the blue, "I think I'll call you Beth."

"Why Beth?" Jane asked reluctantly.

"It was my late granddaughter's name, and I've decided that you remind me of her." A rare shadow drifted across Addie's features, and her smile seemed to falter a little as she met Jane's gaze. "I think she'd like you to have her name. It suits you."

And somehow it did. Somehow, in just saying the name aloud, she became Beth, and it was a relief to let go of Jane Doe, a woman with no name, no memory, no past. She had a real name now, a real life, and because of Addie, the future didn't seem quite as terrifying as it once had.

And then the police came.

They were waiting for her one day when she returned from physical therapy—a young detective and his older sidekick. Addie was nowhere in sight. The nurse who helped Beth back to bed said the older woman had asked to be taken for a walk, but Beth suspected Addie's absence had been arranged by the police.

"I'm Detective MacMillan," the younger one told her. He was tall and lanky with a nice smile and a soft-spoken approach designed to put her at ease. It didn't. "This is my partner, Sergeant Marsden. We've come to help you if we can." He nodded toward the second man, who remained just inside the doorway.

Beth glanced apprehensively at the other detective, a burly, middle-aged man with bitter lips and a hard, seasoned gaze that measured her mercilessly from across the room. When he bent to set his briefcase on the floor, his suit jacket gaped, revealing a gun tucked into a shoulder holster.

There was something about him, a hint of cruelty in his eyes, that made Beth nervous, frightened even.

She was glad he seemed content to keep his distance and let the taller, younger man do all the talking.

"The doctor says you're doing much better." Mac-Millan took a pen from his jacket pocket and flipped open his notebook. "All right if we ask you a few questions?"

"Yes, but...I don't know if I'll be able to answer them."

"Let's give it a shot anyway." He glanced around. "Mind if I sit?" When she shook her head, he pulled up a chair next to her bed. "Dr. Wesley told us you have amnesia. Pretty ironic, isn't it? Here Marsden and I have been waiting around for you to come out of your coma so you could tell us who you are and why you were in such a hurry to get down the mountain that night, and now that you're finally awake, you don't remember what happened."

When she said nothing in response, he cocked his head. "You don't remember *anything?*"

"No."

"Nothing at all? You have no idea who you are?"
She shook her head.

He sighed. "Well, that's a real problem, because no one else seems to know anything about you, either. Any identification you were carrying—driver's license, credit cards—must have been lost in the crash. Or in the river." He paused, studying her with a pensive frown. "It's a little strange, though. You've been in the hospital for, what? Three weeks? The nurses tell us that not one single person has been here asking about you. No one's called or been by the police station to report you missing, either. It's as if you appeared out of the blue on the mountain that night."

He wasn't the first to wonder about her situation. Beth had asked herself the same questions over and over. Had her life been so inconsequential that she could disappear for three weeks and not be missed? Was there no one in her life who cared enough to come looking for her?

"Of course," the detective continued, "we assume you're not from around here, since we couldn't find anybody who recognized your photograph. Maybe you came to the mountains on vacation. That could explain why no one has reported you missing yet. But if you were staying somewhere around here, you'd think someone—a leasing agent, a gas station attendant, a grocery store clerk—*someone* would have seen you. But we've been to lodges, hotels, private homes—you name it—all up and down the mountain. So far we've come up with zip." He scratched his head as if stymied.

Marsden said from the doorway, "Maybe she came up here to meet someone."

MacMillan looked up, as if annoyed by the interruption. "So?"

"If she came up here to meet a boyfriend or girlfriend, whatever—" the cop shrugged, as if her sexual orientation was of no consequence to him "—it could be that her companion came up ahead of her and made all the arrangements. Booked the room or leased a house. Bought the groceries. All she did was show up." He nodded toward Beth.

MacMillan seemed to mull over the possibility. Then he shook his head. "That still doesn't make sense. Why wouldn't her companion have come forward to report her missing?"

"Maybe he—or she—can't come forward."

"Meaning?"

Marsden's cold gaze met Beth's. "Maybe they had a falling out. Maybe something happened that night. Maybe that's why she was out on that mountain road, alone, in a rainstorm."

The way he spoke about her as if she wasn't in the room annoyed her at first, but then fear shot through her. Suddenly, she knew what this was about. Why they were here. They hadn't come to help her. They were here because they thought she'd done something wrong. Something criminal.

She gazed up at Detective MacMillan. In spite of his easygoing demeanor, she knew this was no casual interview. This was a police interrogation and she was a suspect. Everything they'd said to her had been carefully orchestrated before they'd entered her room. They were leading her exactly where they wanted her to go. Where that was she had no idea, but she knew, without a doubt, she was in big trouble.

Her heart started to pound in slow, torturous beats, but even through her fear, the instinct to survive prevailed. She had to be very, very careful here. She couldn't say or do anything to arouse their suspicion any more than it already was. They had the power to arrest her, lock her up in jail, and she would have no way of proving her innocence.

Was she innocent?

"What is it you think I've done?" she asked in a near whisper.

MacMillan shrugged. "We're just trying to find out who you are, for starters. So far, we've come up with more questions than answers. You were brought into this hospital with no ID of any kind. You woke up from a coma with no memory. You can see why we're more than a little curious.''

''What about the car?'' she asked suddenly. ''The license plate or registration—''

''Your car is at the bottom of the river, buried underneath several tons of muck. The storm triggered a mudslide that night. Another few hours and the rescue workers wouldn't have been able to reach you.''

''So…there's nothing to tell you who I am?'' She didn't know whether to be relieved or fearful.

''Not exactly.'' MacMillan nodded toward his partner, who picked up the briefcase and handed it to him. ''One of the first officers at the accident scene found this near the top of the embankment where your car went over.''

She frowned. ''You think it's mine?''

''Oh, it's yours all right. Or at least, it was in your possession at some point.''

Something in his tone caused her heart to beat even harder. ''How do you know?''

''When it was thrown from the car, it landed beneath a rocky ledge that protected it from the storm. We were able to lift a fingerprint from one of the metal latches. The print matches yours.''

Beneath the covers, her hands began to tremble.

''We ran your prints through the national database,'' he said. ''No hits. We also contacted NCIC— the National Crime Information Center—but nothing turned up there, either. In other words, we've found no evidence of a criminal record. Except for this.'' He flipped open the metal latches on the briefcase and drew back the lid so that she could view the contents.

For one agonizing moment, she could hardly catch her breath as she stared at the stacks of money.

"Ten thousand dollars," he told her. "Small denominations, serial numbers clean. We can't match them to any known robberies or heists. We also found this." He removed a gun, protected in a plastic evidence bag, from the bottom of the briefcase. "A .38 special, serial number completely filed away."

Her stomach churned sickeningly.

"Any of this jog your memory?" MacMillan queried.

She shook her head.

"Didn't think so." He closed the briefcase and stood. "Well, I guess that's all we can do for now. We'll be in touch. And in the meantime, if you get your memory back, you call us."

He moved away from the bed, but before he got to the door, he turned, as if an idea had suddenly dawned on him. He took a step toward her. "Oh, and one other thing you should know. The man who pulled you from the river that night said he saw two sets of headlights on the mountain. One set was lower to the ground, presumably on your car. The other lights looked as if they were on a truck or SUV. He said for a few seconds the two sets of lights were traveling side by side down the mountain. Then your car went into a spin and slid over the side. He had the impression that you may have been forced over."

She gasped. "You mean someone...tried to kill me?"

"We don't know for sure what happened. All we can do is speculate. It's been my experience, though, that women don't usually go out alone in the dead of night—much less in a driving rainstorm—just for the hell of it. Something happened on that mountain. You were running from something. Or someone. I'd stake my life on it.''

A .38 special, serial number completely filed away.
Ten thousand dollars. Small denominations…
You were running from something. Or someone.

"Do I need a lawyer?" she asked hoarsely.

MacMillan seemed surprised by the question. "We don't even have evidence that a crime has been committed, unless you know something we don't. But then, even if you did, you wouldn't remember it, would you?" Something she could only name as suspicion gleamed in his eyes, making her tremble even more.

I didn't do anything, she wanted to tell him, but how could she know that for sure? How could she defend herself when she didn't know who she was or what kind of person she'd been? Was she capable of violence? Deception? Betrayal? She had no idea.

As if reading the terror and confusion in her eyes, the detective nodded. "Quite a predicament, isn't it? If someone did try to kill you on that mountain and he finds out you're still alive, he could come looking for you. And if Marsden and I find out you stole that money or used that gun, *we'll* come looking for you." His gaze hardened. "Either way, I'd say you're in one hell of a mess."

CHAPTER TWO

Two years later...

EVERY EVENING after dinner, Beth Young played the piano for the guests at the Twin Oaks Bed and Breakfast in Cooper's Corner, Massachusetts. And every evening when she played, time stood still for Clint Cooper.

Which was strange, because he didn't even like her kind of music. He'd never been fond of those mournful, melancholy refrains she seemed to favor. He and his late wife, Kristin, had been avid patrons of the symphony in New York, but that had been more her passion than his. Deep down, Clint preferred more earthy music. Jazz. Blues. Rock and roll. Something soulful, but not melancholy. Music that stirred passions, not yearning. Clint wasn't the yearning type.

No, Beth's music wasn't at all to his taste, but he had to admit her melodies had a way of haunting him at the most inopportune times. *She* haunted him. He couldn't get her out of his head. Ever since he and his sister, Maureen, had decided to move their families to Cooper's Corner and convert their inherited farmhouse into a bed-and-breakfast, Clint had been drawn to the quiet librarian. She was the first woman who had caught his attention since Kristin's death almost three years ago.

That was also strange, because not only was Beth's music not to his liking, she wasn't particularly his type. He'd always gone for more outgoing, athletic women. Women like his late wife.

Kristin had been a successful art critic who'd possessed the charm and poise necessary to move effortlessly through the snobbish circles of the avant-garde art world in New York, but she'd also been an accomplished horsewoman and champion downhill skier. There was nothing—and no one—she hadn't been able to conquer once she'd set her mind to it.

Beth was...gentle. That was the word that always came to mind when Clint thought of her. He couldn't picture her astride a horse, let alone racing at breakneck speed down a black-diamond ski slope. Nor could he imagine her hobnobbing with the artsy crowd in SoHo or the rich and trendy in Tribeca.

But she wasn't without her own quiet allure, especially with her beautiful dark hair, streaked white at the widow's peak, and those wide, pensive eyes that reminded Clint of liquid violets.

He studied her from his unobtrusive position behind the registration desk, wondering again where her music came from, what drove her to play such sorrowful tunes. Had she been hurt in the past? Disillusioned? Betrayed? Deceived by a lover she'd been devoted to?

What was her story?

He still knew very little about her, even though she'd lived in Cooper's Corner for two years now. She was the town librarian, lived alone in a small cottage on School Street and played the piano exceptionally well. Beyond that, she was a mystery to Clint. An occasional fantasy.

Watching her hands move fluidly over the keys, he found himself indulging in one of those fantasies now, imagining those sensuous fingers stroking his face, trailing down his bare chest until...

"Clint, what do you think you're doing?"

The admonishment, so in sync with his thoughts, caused him to start guiltily. He pretended to be absorbed in the computer screen before looking up. "Oh, hey, Maureen. I didn't hear you come in."

His sister glanced around the gathering room, where guests of the inn and a few people from the village sat enthralled as Beth played. "No, I don't imagine you did. You seemed quite preoccupied."

He shrugged. "It's all these damn bills. They keep piling up...."

She gave him a knowing smile. "You weren't thinking about bills. Not with that look on your face."

He actually had to struggle to keep from blushing. "I don't know what you're talking about."

Maureen came around the desk and stood beside him. "Let me see if I can clarify it for you then. All last fall and winter, when Beth came here to play for the guests at teatime, you frequently found an excuse to be at this desk in the afternoon. Now that she's coming to play after dinner, here you are. It doesn't take a genius to put two and two together."

He arched a brow. "And you think you've got it all figured out, do you, Sherlock?"

"It's elementary, my dear brother. You've got a

thing for Beth Young. What I *can't* figure out is why you don't just ask her out.''

''Who says I want to ask her out?''

''Oh, please, it's as plain as the nose on your face.'' Maureen planted her hands on her hips. ''Don't be such a weenie about it. Just march over there and ask her to dinner. I bet she says yes.''

Clint wasn't so sure about that. Beth was friendly whenever they met up at the B and B or in town, but she was nice to everyone. She'd never given the slightest indication that she thought of him…in the way he thought about her.

''I think it would be great if you two hooked up.'' Maureen's eyes shone as she warmed to the idea. ''I like Beth, and besides, how long has it been since you've had a real date?''

''I could ask you the same thing.''

She sniffed. ''That's different.''

''How is it different?''

''Because…it just is,'' she said impatiently. ''You were married for a long time. You know what a relationship can be like when it works. I would think you'd want to find that again with someone else. But my experience with a serious relationship was a little less pleasant.''

''Oh, I don't know. I seem to recall a time when you and Chance Maguire were pretty hot and heavy,'' Clint murmured.

''Maybe. A long time ago.'' Maureen lifted her chin. ''But I don't want to talk about my ex.''

He shrugged. ''Fair enough. And I don't want to talk about my social life.''

"But that's just the point. If you actually had a social life, we wouldn't have to talk about it."

"Oh, right," he said dryly. "If I know you—and I think I do—you'd want all the gory details."

"You make me sound like Philo and Phyllis," she complained, referring to their distant cousins who ran the local grocery and hardware store and were known affectionately—and sometimes not so affection-ately—as the town gossips. "I'm not like that. I'm just…concerned. I want you to be happy."

"But I'm not unhappy with the way things are now," he argued.

"Life's too short to settle for not being *unhappy.*"

He sighed wearily. "You're not going to let this go, are you?"

She smiled in that superior way she had when she knew she was winning an argument. "No, because I'm right. You let a good thing pass you by, and you could end up regretting it for the rest of your life." She paused, her expression softening a bit. "I know it must be hard to let go of what you and Kristin had. You two had the perfect marriage. But she's gone now—"

"Don't say that," he snapped.

Maureen looked stricken. "Oh, Clint, I'm sorry. I should have realized—"

"No marriage is perfect," he said bitterly.

"Well, no…of course not." His sister seemed mo-mentarily confused, as if they were talking about two different things. "But what you and Kristin had…"

Was a lie, he almost blurted, but he caught himself and gritted his teeth before responding. "We had twelve years together, but that's over. I'm not living in the past. If I've decided to go it alone, it's not because of my grief.''

His disillusionment with his late wife was still something he couldn't bring himself to talk about. All their friends and family had assumed, as Maureen had, that he and Kristin had had the ideal marriage. Hell, Clint had thought so, too, once. They were perfect for each other. Everyone said so.

It was only in looking back after her death that he'd realized how far from perfection they'd strayed. That all the little signs of discontent had been there for years, but he'd chosen to ignore them because it was easier to pretend they didn't exist than to deal with them.

But when she'd died, he could no longer hide from the truth. He'd gone looking for answers, and he'd found secrets, dark ones. Secrets that had almost destroyed him and cost him his son. He'd sworn then that he would never be duped again, not by anyone. But especially not by love.

''Look,'' he said. ''I know you mean well, but even if I wanted to date, which I don't, I wouldn't have the time. We're both putting in a lot of hours around this place, and I've got a son to raise. I almost screwed that up once. I'm not about to let it happen again.''

''But Keegan's doing great,'' Maureen protested.

''And I intend to keep it that way. Besides, if I go off on some date, who's going to keep an eye on you?'' Clint was only half joking, and although Maureen gave him an exasperated look, he saw her mouth tighten. She was more worried about her own situation than she liked to let on. They both were.

Before they'd moved to Cooper's Corner, she'd been a detective with the NYPD. She and her partner, Dan D'Angelo, had busted a creep named Carl Nevil for murder, and their testimony had helped send him to a maximum security prison for the rest of his life. Unfortunately, Owen Nevil, a convicted felon in his own right, had been released on parole soon after his brother's incarceration. They'd sworn revenge on the cops who'd put Carl behind bars, and there'd been enough close calls in the city to convince Maureen, Dan and their superior, Frank Quigg, that the Nevils meant business.

If it had been only her own life on the line, Clint knew that Maureen would never have given up the job she loved. She would have stayed and faced the danger. But she had her little girls to consider. She decided it was best to get the twins out of the city, and it hadn't taken much to convince Clint that he and Keegan would be better off in Cooper's Corner as well.

Their hope had been that a small town in Massachusetts would be the last place Owen Nevil would think to look for Maureen, but certain incidents in the last several months had left her and Clint on edge. They were convinced Nevil knew Maureen was in Cooper's Corner, and he was toying with her in some sick game of cat and mouse until he was ready to make his final move.

As if revisiting the dangers in her own mind, Maureen said suddenly, "Have you seen the twins—" She broke off, putting a finger to her lips as a muffled snigger came from behind a nearby curtain.

Tiptoeing to one of the long windows that looked

out on the front lawn, she whisked back the drapes, revealing two little auburn-haired imps, pudgy hands clapped tightly to their mouths to smother their giggles.

"And just what have we here?" Maureen knelt and started tickling the girls' ribs until their laughter erupted and turned into high-pitched squeals that might have drowned out Beth's music if she hadn't already finished her set.

"So tell me," Maureen said, giving each girl a loud smooch on the cheek. "What are you two doing hiding behind the curtains?"

Robin said brightly, "We're spying on Uncle Clint."

Randi turned to her sister in disgust. "You talk too much, you stupid pigeon."

"Do not!"

"Do, too!"

"Randi," Maureen admonished. "We don't call each other names. You know better than that. And besides, I think the term you're looking for is stool pigeon."

"See?" Randi said in triumph. "Even Mommy knows you're a stupid stool pigeon."

"Am not!"

"Are, too!"

"Girls." Maureen folded her arms. "Maybe we'd better get to the bottom of this spy business before someone gets herself in trouble." She glanced pointedly at Randi. "Why are you spying on Uncle Clint?"

"We can't tell you." Randi folded her arms in a perfect imitation of her mother.

"Yeah, we can't tell you." Robin crossed her arms, too, but she looked as if she were itching to tell.

Clint came over and knelt beside Maureen. "Did I hear right? I'm the target of two international secret agents? What are you after? The classified documents I have stashed under my mattress?"

Robin giggled and shook her head.

"The super-duper decoder ring I keep under my pillow?"

"No!"

"Hmm." He rubbed his chin. "What could it be, I wonder."

"We promised we wouldn't tell," Randi said, glowering at her sister.

"Yeah, we promised," Robin agreed.

"And you made that promise to whom?" Maureen inquired innocently.

"Keegan," Robin said without hesitation.

"Stupid pigeon," Randi muttered darkly.

"Why does Keegan want you to spy on me?" Clint asked.

Both little girls lifted their shoulders.

"Do you know where he is now?"

"Outside," Robin said.

"What's he doing outside?"

"Spying on Miss Young." Having cracked under the pressure, Robin decided to sing like a canary. All poor Randi could do was give her dirty looks.

"Why on earth is he spying on Beth Young?" Maureen inquired.

Damn good question.

"We don't know." Robin stared up at Clint, all

wide-eyed innocence. "Uncle Clint? Do you think Miss Young's pretty?"

That took him by surprise. "Uh, yeah, I guess so."

"Do you want to be her boyfriend?"

"Robin!" Maureen scolded, but she could barely suppress a smile. "We don't ask people, even Uncle Clint, such personal questions."

Oh, yeah? Since when? He shot Maureen a look, which she chose to ignore, much as Robin was ignoring Randi's murderous glare.

Clint ruffled Robin's hair. "What do you know about boyfriends, anyway?"

"She knows everything about boyfriends," Randi answered smugly, "because she has one!"

"I do not!" Robin hotly declared.

"Do, too!"

"Do not!"

"Okay, that's enough." Maureen took each of them by the hand and pointed them toward the hallway that led to their private suite at the back of the house. "You guys are way too cranky tonight. It's bathtime, and then I'm putting you both to bed."

"Without a story?" Randi complained

"Yeah, without a story?" bemoaned her echo.

"Depends on how much cooperation I get while you're in the tub," Maureen warned.

"We want to hear about Max Danger," Randi declared.

Clint lifted a brow. "Who on earth is Max Danger?"

"Disney's version of James Bond," Maureen explained.

"He's the bestest spy in the whole wide world,"

Randi elaborated. "And he has a real badass car and—"

"Randi!" Maureen gasped. "Where did you hear such language?"

"Keegan," Robin, the informant, happily told her. "He says it all the time."

Oh, hell, Clint thought.

Maureen shot him a glance, and he mouthed quickly, *I'll talk to him.*

She turned back to the girls, who were still chattering away about Keegan and Max Danger and a car that could go "underwater like a sub boat and fly through the air like a copter." It was hard to determine whether their hero-worship was heaped more lavishly upon Keegan or Max Danger.

They ran on ahead as Maureen walked back over to the desk where Clint had retreated.

"I'll talk to Keegan about his language," he promised, trying to head her off. "I'm going out right now to find him."

"I'd appreciate that. Those two are a handful as it is." She let out a weary sigh. "God help me. They're barely four and already their heads can be turned by a guy with a cool car."

"Wonder who they get that from?"

"What?" Her gaze narrowed suspiciously.

Clint shrugged. "Nothing. I was just trying to remember what kind of car Chance drove when you two met."

"Oh, go ahead and have your fun," Maureen warned irritably. "But just remember, I'm not the one whose kid is going to want one of those badass cars in a couple of years."

She tossed her head as she walked away, and Clint had to give her credit. As a parting shot, it was a good one.

The image of Keegan behind the wheel of a muscle car—and Keegan would want a muscle car—was enough to keep Clint tossing and turning until his son turned thirty.

It was almost as worrisome as the notion of Keegan outside somewhere, spying on Beth Young.

Clint headed for the front door with grim resolve. What the hell was that kid up to now?

CHAPTER THREE

"CAN YOU STILL SEE HER?" Bryan Penrose called up in a loud whisper. "I don't hear the piano anymore. What's she doing?"

Keegan hitched himself up to the high windowsill and peered through the pane again. "She's stopped playing, and now she's just standing around talking to some people."

"What about your dad? Do you see him?"

"Uh-uh. I think he must still be at the front desk. I can't see it from here."

"Why do you suppose the twins didn't report back?" Bryan wondered as he bent and scratched behind his knee. "Think they got caught?"

"Yeah, probably." Keegan hadn't expected much help from that quarter, anyway. He'd sent his cousins off to spy on his dad mainly just to get rid of them. They were cute and all, and most of the time he enjoyed playing with them. But sometimes they could be a real pain, like when they asked a million questions. "Watch out, I'm coming down." He dropped easily to the ground and brushed off his hands.

Glancing around to make sure they were still alone, Keegan said in a conspiratorial tone, "Okay, here's the plan. I'll sneak in the back way so my dad doesn't see me, and then I'll go up to Miss Young and start

talking to her about books or something so she
doesn't leave. Then you go find my dad and tell him
I need to see him. Say it's, like, urgent or something.
When he comes to find me in the gathering room, I'll
be there with Miss Young.''

Bryan shook his head. ''I still don't get it. You're
going to all this trouble just so your dad will talk to
Miss Young?''

Keegan rolled his eyes. ''Not just so they'll talk,
dork. So they'll, you know, go out and stuff.''

''Yeah, but why do you care if they go out? Why
don't you just let your dad find his own girlfriend?''

''Because he won't.''

''Why not?''

Keegan shrugged. ''I don't know. I guess he thinks
he has to spend all his spare time with me. You know,
because of what happened in New York.''

Bryan nodded solemnly. ''On account of your being in the 'hood and all.''

''I wasn't in a gang,'' Keegan said angrily. ''That's
just a stupid rumor.'' But it was a rumor that hit a
little too close to home. While he hadn't exactly gone
so far as to join a street gang in New York, he'd
considered it, and his reckless actions had gotten him
into plenty of trouble, both at home and at school.
Keegan didn't much like thinking about those days
now, but he knew his dad still thought about them a
lot and worried that Keegan would turn out bad, even
though he'd made new friends in Cooper's Corner
and his grades were a lot better.

Keegan figured all parents worried about their kids,
but it made him feel guilty to think of his dad putting

his own life on hold because he was afraid Keegan would slip back into his old habits.

He'd been mixed up and miserable after his mother died, but he was older now. He knew how to stay out of trouble, and it was time his dad forgot all the bad stuff he'd done. He wanted his dad to be happy, have some fun, but the only way that was going to happen was if he had something—or someone—other than Keegan to focus his attention on.

Keegan just hoped Miss Young worked out better than all the other women he'd picked for his dad, because the clock was ticking. At thirty-six, his father wasn't getting any younger, and Keegan was fast running out of eligible women in Cooper's Corner.

"Keegan! You out here?"

"Uh-oh, that's your dad," Bryan warned needlessly. "And he sounds mad."

"No sh—"

"*Keegan!*"

BETH SMILED POLITELY as she made small talk with two of the guests from the inn. Although an introvert, she usually enjoyed meeting new people and interacting with the folks from the village who came to Twin Oaks to hear her play. Tonight, though, all she wanted to do was make a quick getaway before anyone noticed how upset she was.

Actually, she was more than upset. She was terrified. When she'd glimpsed that face in the window above the piano, her heart had almost stopped. Her fingers had faltered badly on the keys, and even now she wasn't sure how she'd been able to recover, how she'd managed to continue when her hands had been shaking so badly.

They were still shaking. She didn't dare accept the cup of tea someone offered her, though it was exactly the fortification she needed. No, she had to get out of there. Tea would come later, when she was alone, safe and sound behind locked doors.

And just when things had been going so well. Just when she'd almost been able to pretend that her life was normal. That her past was never going to catch up with her. That she might not be in danger, after all.

She should have known she was living in a fool's paradise. Too many things had happened around town in the past year. A guest at Twin Oaks had been shot. A horse in the Christmas parade had bolted, endangering Grace McCabe and her daughter. Maureen had been run off the road by a truck. None of those events were directly related to Beth, of course, but she couldn't help wondering if she was somehow responsible for them. If she had inadvertently brought danger to the sleepy little town of Cooper's Corner.

She'd tried to tell herself that it was all just some strange coincidence. After all, she'd been here for well over a year before bad things had started to happen. She was still safe here. No one could find her. The faces she saw lurking in shadows were nothing more than her imagination.

But the face in the window tonight had been all too real.

She'd had only a glimpse, a mere impression of eyes staring at her from the darkness, but she'd known without a doubt that someone was out there. Someone was watching her.

Excusing herself now from the small group that had gathered around her, she hurried across the room toward the front entrance. It was a warm July night so she didn't have to worry about retrieving a coat. She'd just slip out unobtrusively and no one would miss her.

The registration desk was unoccupied, and Beth breathed a sigh of relief. She liked Maureen Cooper and got along well with her, but something about the woman made her uncomfortable. Beth always had a strange feeling that Maureen could see right through her. That she knew Beth was a fraud, but, for whatever reason, had decided not to blow the whistle on her…yet.

And then there was Maureen's brother, Clint. At the mere thought of him, Beth's heart started to race. She didn't want to feel such a powerful attraction to him, or to any man, but she couldn't seem to help herself. Ever since he'd come into the library last winter to check out the latest Tom Clancy novel, Beth hadn't been able to get him out of her head.

Oh, she saw him all the time, of course, at Twin Oaks and in town. But somehow that day at the library had been different. Somehow, with snow falling outside and no one around but the two of them, Beth's awareness of him had been heightened. And when his fingers had brushed hers as she handed the book over the counter—

Electric. That was the only way to describe the moment, the sensation, the thrill after thrill that had coursed through her body.

Whether he'd noticed or not, Beth had no idea. He'd given her no indication that he had, other than a polite smile, although she wanted to believe that his gaze had lingered. That there'd been a spark, no matter how tiny, flickering in the depths of his forest-green eyes.

Ever since that day, Beth had found herself thinking about him constantly, dreaming about him. But even if by some miracle he did feel the same attraction for her, nothing could come of it. She wasn't free to fall in love.

Not even with a man like Clint Cooper.

Especially not with Clint Cooper. He had a son, and Beth would never knowingly put a child in danger, no matter how much she might yearn for a family.

The terrible loneliness since Addie's death two years ago welled inside her, and for a moment, hot tears scalded her eyes. Then she brushed them away as she always did. What good did crying do? It made one weak and vulnerable, but it changed nothing. Better to just get on with the life she and Addie had created for her than to dwell on the one that had been lost, or the one that was never going to be.

She opened the door, intent on fleeing into the night, but a shadow loomed before her, and in the split second before they collided, one thought flashed through Beth's mind. If ever she'd been given a portent of coming danger, it was the sight of Clint Cooper, a protective arm thrown over his son's shoulders, blocking her escape.

"HEY, YOU OKAY?" He put both hands on her arms to steady her, and a rush of sensations stormed through Beth's body. She felt tingly all over from even so small a contact.

"Yes, I'm fine," she managed to say breathlessly. "I wasn't looking where I was going, I guess." She glanced at Keegan. "Hello, Keegan."

"Hi, Miss Young."

"You did seem in a hurry." Clint's green eyes darkened. "Everything okay?"

No, Beth thought shakily. Everything wasn't okay. Someone had been staring at her through the window. Someone who might want to harm her, who might threaten her very existence. But even as the thought formed in her head, the potential danger of the situation seemed to lose urgency as Clint continued to stare down at her. As his hands tightened ever so slightly on her arms to steady her.

That was one of the things about him she found so desirable, Beth thought fleetingly. His steadiness. His strength. He would be a rock in the face of disaster, and she couldn't deny the appeal of having such an anchor in her life.

But she couldn't deny the physical attraction, either. The purely visceral reaction she had every time she saw him. He had the most amazing green eyes, the kind she could stare into forever, and thick, chestnut hair that called out to her fingers. And he was so tall! And so...masculine. He'd done a lot of the renovation work on Twin Oaks himself, and the physical labor showed in the tanned muscles of his arms and shoulders, in his broad, solid chest and flat stomach.

He was the perfect man, Beth thought with an inward sigh. But he was not the man for her. No man was.

"Beth?" His gaze was still on her, but his expression had changed. He looked worried. "Are you sure you're okay?"

She forced a smile. "I'm just tired. It's been a long day, and I'm ready to go home."

Something flickered in his eyes, an emotion she wanted to believe was disappointment. "We won't keep you then."

Beside him, Keegan cleared his throat. "Uh, it's getting pretty late, Dad." He cut a glance toward Beth.

Something dawned in Clint's face as he and his son exchanged knowing looks. Clint turned back to Beth. "I didn't see your car out front. Do you need a lift home?"

The thought of being alone with Clint made Beth's pulse race faster. "Thanks, but I'm parked at the end of the driveway. I didn't want to be in the way. Looks like you have a full house this weekend."

"Yeah, we've been pretty lucky since we opened. Knock on wood." He smiled.

"Well…good night…."

Keegan said unexpectedly, "It's really dark out there, Dad. You said so yourself." His nod toward the door was almost imperceptible, but Clint seemed to understand. The silent exchange between father and son was a bit disconcerting for Beth. Was this the way all families communicated?

"Someone should probably walk you to your car," Clint murmured.

"Oh, that's really not—"

"I promised Aunt Maureen I'd help out with the twins," Keegan piped up, cutting off Beth's protest.

"Good night, Miss Young."

"Good night, Keegan. I hope to see you again at the library before long."

It might have been her imagination—or else poor lighting in the foyer—but Beth could have sworn Keegan blushed furiously before he hurried off toward the hallway.

"Keegan?" Clint called after him. When the boy turned, his father said, "We'll continue our conversation later."

Keegan glanced from Clint to Beth and then back to Clint. Something odd gleamed in his eyes. "Sure, Dad."

Beth couldn't help but feel there was something going on here she didn't understand. Reluctantly, she turned to Clint. "Look, you really don't—"

"Humor me," he said with a smile. "I could use some fresh air."

She didn't protest further because she didn't much relish walking alone down the dark driveway to her car.

The night was so silent that the click of the closing door behind them caused her to jump, but she knew that the company, and not the noise, was the cause of her nerves.

Her reaction to him was like that of a schoolgirl with a silly crush, she thought. But in a very real sense, Clint Cooper *was* her first crush. For all she knew, she'd had lots of men in her life before the accident, but she couldn't remember any of them. She had no recollection of ever having felt this way about a man before.

"Nice night," Clint said beside her. He took her elbow as they descended the steps, and Beth closed her eyes briefly.

Her shoulder brushed a spray of roses, stirring the sweet, dreamy scent, and something that might have been a memory drifted through her. She couldn't remember being with a man, being in love, but she knew what it was like. She knew why her heart pounded when Clint looked at her the way he did and why her stomach fluttered in awareness when he touched her. She knew why she felt breathless at his nearness.

"Look at that sky," he said in awe as they moved side by side down the walkway toward the drive.

Beth tipped her face up to the star-drenched heavens. The sky seemed almost magical tonight, as if anything might happen. She wouldn't have been surprised to see a shooting star. "It's beautiful," she said softly.

"That sky was one of the things I missed most when my family moved to the city," he said. "Although after a while, you forget about the stars. And then you come out here, to a place like this, and you realize what you've been missing all these years."

Was there a deeper meaning in his words? Beth shivered, thinking about the possibilities. "Moving back here must have been something of a culture shock, though. Do you ever miss the city?"

"Sometimes," he admitted. "New York gets under your skin. There's no place like it."

"Why did you leave?"

He shrugged. "I've always been a small-town guy at heart, and besides, it was time for a change." They were at the end of the walkway, and he took her elbow to steer her toward the long drive lined with oak trees.

It wasn't that he thought she needed guidance, Beth thought. Taking her arm was merely a reflex for him. An old-fashioned, courtly gesture that was so deeply ingrained in his psyche he probably wasn't even aware of what he was doing. Beth didn't mind. There was nothing condescending in Clint's manner toward her, and besides, she liked the feel of his hand on her arm.

"After my wife died, Keegan and I went through a hard time," he said. "He fell in with a bad crowd, and by the time I realized what was going on, it was almost too late. He was in serious trouble. I had to do something drastic or lose my son forever."

"So you gave up your career, your home, everything, and moved here."

"It wasn't much of a sacrifice. Not considering what I got in return. I haven't regretted the decision once."

Beth wished she could see his expression, wished she could know what he was thinking. "Keegan's a good kid. He's so polite and respectful when he comes into the library."

Clint paused, staring down at her. "He comes to the library a lot, does he?"

"A couple of times a week lately. It's nice to see a boy his age show an interest in books instead of obsessing over video games and MTV."

Clint tilted his head. "We're talking about Keegan Cooper, right?"

Beth laughed. "You didn't know he liked to read?"

"News to me. They say the parent is always the last to know."

"At least he's into books and not drugs," Beth pointed out.

"Amen to that."

They started walking again, and it seemed to Beth that the exchange had lightened the mood. She began to relax, but as they neared the end of the drive, a thought suddenly occurred to her. What would happen when they got to her car? How should she handle her exit? Did she simply thank him for his thoughtfulness and then leave? Did she offer him her hand?

Her heart started to knock painfully against her chest. What if he tried to kiss her good-night?

No, that was crazy. He wouldn't do that. Why would he?

But once the notion was planted in her head, Beth couldn't get rid of it. All she could think about was Clint leaning toward her, brushing his lips against hers, and then—

"What about you?"

She jumped at the sound of his voice. "Excuse me?"

"I know you've been in Cooper's Corner for a couple of years, but where are you from originally?"

The question was like a dousing of cold water. Her romantic fantasies fizzled in the face of her own reality. "I moved here from California."

He laughed softly, in surprise. "Somehow I never would have pegged you for a California girl. You don't seem the type, and I mean that in the nicest way." She knew he was teasing her, and she wanted to respond in kind, but questions about her past made her freeze up. Terrified her.

It wasn't that she wanted to be secretive. On more than one occasion she'd considered telling the people she'd grown so fond of in Cooper's Corner the truth. *I don't know where I'm from. I don't even know who I am. I'm not really Beth Young, you see. That name was given to me by a woman I met in the hospital while I was recovering from a terrible automobile accident. I was in a coma for three weeks, and when I woke up, I had amnesia. I don't know anything about my past except that I had a briefcase full of money in my car and a gun that had been fired twice. The police think I stole that money. They suspect I may have shot someone. I could be a criminal or a...murderer. There's really no telling what kind of person I was in my previous life. Oh, and one other thing. Someone may want to kill me....*

She tried to imagine the expression on Clint's face if she blurted all that out to him now.

"Did you grow up in California?"

She wavered. "I...don't really like to talk about my childhood."

"I'm sorry. I didn't mean to pry." He sounded genuinely regretful, but he didn't bother trying to hide his curiosity. "It's just that, despite all the times you've been at Twin Oaks, I suddenly realized I know hardly anything about you. Odd, for a small town."

"Here's my car," she said in a rush, and thrust out her hand. "Thank you for walking me out."

He hesitated, as if her gesture caught him by surprise, but then he took her hand in his and held it for a long, tingling moment. "No problem. It was the least I could do. I still think we should be paying you to play for us. It doesn't seem right that you give up your evenings without compensation.''

"I told you, I don't play for money. I play for pleasure. And anyway, you're the one doing me a favor. If you didn't let me use the piano, I would never get to play.''

"That *would* be a shame,'' he murmured. He was still holding her hand, and it seemed to Beth that he moved toward her ever so slightly. At five-eight, she was a tall woman, but he towered over her by at least six inches. He was an impressive man, she thought breathlessly. In more ways than one.

His gaze deepened and he smiled, a slow, enigmatic smile that suggested a good-night kiss might not be the last thing on his mind, either. But he made no move toward her. Instead he cocked his head, staring down at her as if he couldn't quite figure her out. "Good night, Beth.''

"Good night, Clint.''

It wasn't until she was in her car driving away from Twin Oaks that she was finally able to expel a long, quivering breath.

CHAPTER FOUR

CLINT KNOCKED on Keegan's door, then stuck his head inside. Keegan was sitting at his computer, and Clint could hear him instant-messaging back and forth to a friend. He hoped Keegan was IMing a buddy here in Cooper's Corner and not one of the thugs he'd hung out with in the city.

Keegan had changed so much since their move to Cooper's Corner that he seemed a totally different kid from the surly, rebellious preteen who'd gotten into so much trouble in New York. Clint wanted to trust his son, and most of the time he did. But lately…

He frowned as he stared at his son. Lately Keegan's behavior had been a little puzzling, to say the least. According to Beth, he frequented the library at least twice a week. Innocent enough on the face of it, but it didn't sound like the Keegan Clint knew. And this business about spying on Beth while getting the twins to spy on him. Something odd about that, too. Clint hated to be the suspicious type, but unless he missed his guess, his son was definitely up to something.

Keegan's grin, however, was guileless when he glanced up from his computer. "Hey, Dad."

His smile was so much like his mother's, Clint thought with a pang. Keegan and Kristin had been very close. Whatever else her faults, she'd been a terrific mother. Clint had to give her that. Even with all her secrets, she'd been a better mother to their son than Clint had been a father. Keegan's problems after Kristin's death could be laid squarely at Clint's feet. If he hadn't been so caught up in his own misery, his own regrets—

"Something wrong, Dad?"

Clint forced himself out of his reverie and walked over to sit on Keegan's bed. "Nope. Just thought it might be a good time to finish our conversation."

"Okay." An IM sounded on Keegan's computer, and Clint glanced automatically at the screen. Before he could see anything, however, Keegan touched a key and the screen went blank.

"I want to make sure you understand what I was trying to say to you earlier," Clint said.

Keegan shrugged. "Sure. I need to watch my language around the twins."

"Not just around the twins. I want you to clean up your language, period. Got it?"

"Yes, sir."

"Okay, good. And about this spying stuff—"

"But, Dad, I already told you," Keegan protested. "It was just a stupid game. Bryan and I made the whole thing up so we could get the twins to quit following us around."

"So you sent them to follow me instead," Clint said dryly.

Keegan grinned. "They like you, Dad."

"I know they do, but they look up to you. That's why it's important for you to set a good example for them. And it's especially important that we all keep an eye on them."

Keegan sobered. "Because of that guy that's after Aunt Maureen."

Clint nodded. He'd told Keegan about Owen Nevil after they'd first moved to Cooper's Corner because he thought it important that his son know enough to be alert for possible danger, not just for the twins' sake, but for his own.

"Considering everything that's going on, it's probably not such a hot idea to be playing spy games around here right now," he advised.

"You think Aunt Maureen might think I'm Owen Nevil and shoot me?" Keegan asked, not a bit worried.

"Of course not. But if you and Bryan are lurking behind corners and peeping in windows, you might give her a start, and she doesn't need to be any more stressed than she already is. We have to look out for each other, Keegan."

He nodded eagerly. "I know, Dad. I've been thinking about what you said earlier, and that's why I thought someone should walk Miss Young to her car. She doesn't have anyone to look out for her."

Why this sudden interest in Beth Young? Clint wondered uneasily. He wanted to appreciate his son's thoughtfulness, but Clint couldn't help but worry there might be more to Keegan's motives than met the eye. He stood and put a hand on his son's shoulder. "You're okay with everything we talked about tonight? *We're* okay?"

"Sure, Dad, we're cool."

"Good." But there was something in Keegan's eyes, a hint of the old secretiveness, that worried Clint more than a little.

BETH AWAKENED with a start, catapulted from her sleep by the recurring nightmare that had plagued her since she'd left the hospital two years ago. The dream was always the same. She found herself stumbling around in a fog so thick and dark she couldn't see her hand when she lifted it up to her face. The swirling haze disoriented her so badly she had no sense of direction. She was hopelessly lost.

But she wasn't alone in the fog. Someone was behind her, following her uncannily through the mist, knowing instinctively her every move. She couldn't run fast enough, couldn't hide well enough to elude the nameless, faceless pursuer who wanted her dead. Eventually, she would be found. Beth knew that with a dreaded certainty that tightened like a cold fist around her heart as she ran blindly through the mist.

Somehow, even in her dream, she knew all she had to do to vanquish her fear was turn and face her enemy. But she couldn't make herself do that, not because she was afraid for her life, but because she was terrified of what—or who—she would see.

As always, the nightmare left her drained and vulnerable, and she lay on her back, staring at the ceiling. Beth knew why the nightmare had returned now after months of respite. It was because of Clint Cooper. The dream was her mind's way of warning her that she couldn't get close to him. Not as long as there was a chance she might have a criminal background that could come back to haunt her. Not as long as there was someone out there who might want to kill her.

Her strength returning, Beth got up and walked through her tiny cottage, checking all the doors and windows as she always did after a nightmare. Everything was secure. She was as safe as she could be under the circumstances, and she stored the lingering remnants of the dream exactly where they should be, in the deepest recesses of her mind. She wouldn't get careless, but neither would she live her life in a constant state of panic.

Pausing by the kitchen sink, she poured herself a drink of water and then peered out the window, gazing at the same sky she and Clint had studied together earlier. The night was still and clear, but somehow it seemed to Beth that the glow of the stars had dimmed. Or was it just that in Clint's presence everything seemed brighter and more...alive?

She closed her eyes, remembering the way he'd stared down at her, with starlight in his eyes. Remembering the curve of his lips as he smiled. She didn't recall ever having been kissed in the past, but she knew she must have been because the anticipation had been almost overwhelming. She'd wanted him to kiss her, but she'd also been afraid. Afraid that she would never want him to stop.

Shoving that memory to the back of her mind as well, Beth turned and retraced her steps to the bedroom. But instead of crawling between the covers, she retrieved a small metal box from its hiding place in the closet and flipped open the lock.

Inside was the hospital bracelet that had identified her as Jane Doe, along with articles written about her in the local papers, and the Polaroid the police had taken of her while she lay in a coma.

Beth stared at the photo, hardly able to believe that the pale, still woman was her. Her head was thickly bandaged, and though they weren't visible in the picture, she remembered the tubes and needles attached to her body and to a series of machines that had helped keep her alive.

But of her life before waking up in the hospital, she still remembered nothing.

Why had she been traveling all alone on a treacherous mountain road in a rainstorm? Had she been running away from someone? From something she'd done?

"You're a good person, Beth. I know you didn't do anything wrong," Addie had told her in the hospital after the police's initial visit.

"But you can't know that," Beth fretted. "You don't know anything about me, and neither do I. I could have killed someone—"

"That's impossible," Addie said firmly.

"Then how do you explain the gun, the money...."

Addie gave her a sympathetic smile. "I'm afraid I don't have any easy answers for you, Beth. No one does. But I know you're not a killer. I know you aren't capable of violence. Losing your memory doesn't change the essence of who you are."

"That's not true," Beth said unhappily. "Dr. Wesley told me that severe head trauma can cause drastic changes in personality. How do we know that I wasn't a very different person before the accident?"

"I know the kind of person you are now," Addie insisted. "And as far as I'm concerned, that's all that counts."

Beth wanted to believe that was true. After all, if someone had tried to kill her on that mountain, she was the victim, right? She could have been an innocent bystander who had been at the wrong place at the wrong time.

But the missing bullets in the gun, the caseful of money and the absence of identification on her person suggested otherwise.

And why had no one come looking for her? In the six weeks she'd recuperated in the hospital, no one had reported her missing. The police had been up and down the mountain and in all the nearby towns asking questions. No one had ever seen her before. No one knew anything about her. How could that be? It was almost as if she'd materialized from thin air on the mountainside that night, just as Detective MacMillan had suggested.

But Beth knew that wasn't true. She'd had a life before. A family, maybe. Where were they now? Were they out there somewhere, still looking for her? Did they wonder what had happened to her?

Had one of them tried to kill her?

She'd contacted some of the missing persons bureaus on her own, and a nurse at the hospital had suggested she build a Web site to display her photograph and all her pertinent information. But Detective MacMillan had cautioned against her becoming too proactive on the case.

"You'd be wise to let us handle the investigation. If someone did try to harm you that night, then he or she is still out there. Asking the wrong questions of the wrong people, much less putting up a Web site, could bring the killer straight to your doorstep. What you need to do is find a way to live your life when you get out of here."

Good advice, Beth supposed, but easier said than

done. Where would she go? How would she take care of herself? She had absolutely no idea what skills she'd possessed before the accident, what kind of job she would be able to perform. But Addie had come to her rescue yet again.

"You'll come home with me, of course."

Beth had been shocked by the suggestion. "I can't do that! Aside from the imposition, I could be putting you in danger. If someone is looking for me—"

"I have terminal leukemia, Beth. The doctors have given me three months at best. I'm not afraid of anything except dying alone."

"But I'm afraid for you. If anything happened to you because of me, I'd never be able to forgive myself."

Addie gazed across the space between their two beds. "You think I'm making this offer out of the goodness of my heart, but I'm not. I'm a selfish old woman who has outlived her husband, her son and her only grandchild. My family is dead, Beth. Anyone who's ever been close to me is gone. You need a place to stay until you get your bearings, and I need a friend. I like to think God brought us together so we could help each other."

Beth was touched beyond words by the woman's generosity. And put like that, she didn't have the heart to refuse Addie's offer, so after her release from the hospital, she moved in with the older woman.

Over the next few weeks, she tried to make Addie's remaining time as comfortable as possible. She ran errands, wrote letters and did her best to help put Addie's house and business affairs in order.

And then one day Beth discovered she could play

the piano. Addie was delighted and insisted that Beth
perform for her often. Beth had no idea where her
music came from. She didn't recognize any of the
tunes that flowed so easily from her fingertips, but the
music was there, inside her. And when she played,
for the first time since awakening from her coma she
felt whole again.

One day after an impromptu concert in Addie's
parlor, the older woman asked Beth to retrieve a large
envelope from a handsome walnut desk in the corner.
Dumping the contents of the package in her lap, Addie smiled in satisfaction. "There. Everything you
need to start a new life."

Beth gazed at the documents in confusion. "I don't
understand."

Addie waved her hand over the papers. "It's all
here. My granddaughter's birth certificate, her social
security card, her college diploma. Everything."

Beth gasped in comprehension. "But that would be
stealing her identity. I can't do that."

"You're not stealing it," Addie said firmly. "I'm
giving it to you."

"But that's illegal!"

"Who's to ever know?"

When Beth remained speechless, Addie took her
hand and pulled her down beside her on the sofa.
"You have to have a name, an identification. If the
government has to create one for you, it could take
years and untold red tape. And it would leave a paper
trail for the killer to follow. This way, you can simply
go somewhere far away and become Beth Young. After I'm gone, no one will know but you."

Beth didn't argue further because she didn't want

to upset Addie, but inside she knew she couldn't do
what her friend was asking. Allowing herself to be
called by a dead woman's name was one thing, but
to take that woman's identity, her *life*...

But over the next few days, as she and Addie sorted
through old photographs and the older woman remi-
nisced about the family she'd lost, a strange thing
happened to Beth. Addie painted such vivid pictures
with her words that it was almost as if those memories
became Beth's. The images filled a deep void inside
her, and suddenly she wanted more than anything to
be the real Beth, to have a home and family, someplace to belong.

"When I was a little girl," Addie told her as they
perused one of the older photo albums, "my family
lived in Boston, but we had a summerhouse in the
Berkshires, in a little town called Cooper's Corner.
My best friend in the whole world lived there." She
showed Beth a faded picture of two little girls in
white pinafores standing beneath an oak tree. "The
two of us were inseparable during the summer, closer
even than sisters. When my father moved us out here
to California, I eventually lost touch with Georgia,
but summers I spent in that little town were the
happiest of my life. I've always regretted not going
back." She squeezed Beth's hand. "You can go back
there for me. You can start your new life as Beth
Young in that happy little town, far away from here.
I could rest peacefully, knowing you were there."

So here I am, Beth thought, staring down at the
mementos of her stolen past. And in the two years
she'd been in Cooper's Corner, she had been if not
happy, at least content. She loved her job, her house,

this town. She felt safe here, and although she had no close friends to speak of, she'd made a place for herself in Cooper's Corner. Georgia Cordell, Addie's friend, had persuaded her to stay on when she'd learned that Beth had no other family. She'd helped Beth get a job at the library, taught her everything she knew, and when Georgia retired, she'd persuaded the town council to hire Beth to take her place, even though Beth didn't have the necessary credentials. In Cooper's Corner, Beth soon learned, red tape could be dispensed with in favor of practicality.

That was only one of the things she loved about this place, and she'd come to think that Cooper's Corner really was where she belonged.

But the face in the window tonight had changed all that. It had reminded her that her life was a complete fraud, and that somewhere out there, maybe in this very town, a killer lurked.

A killer, for all Beth knew, who still wanted her dead.

CHAPTER FIVE

AFTER A NIGHT SPENT tossing and turning, Beth was exhausted at work the next day. Even a second cup of coffee at the library and the new catalog from her favorite publishing house couldn't keep her mind from wandering. She couldn't stop thinking about Clint Cooper. When she closed her eyes, she could still see him staring down at her in the starlight, smiling as he contemplated—she was sure—kissing her good-night.

And she'd wanted that kiss. Oh, how she'd wanted that kiss. With very little effort, Beth could imagine the way his lips would feel against hers. Firm but gentle. At least at first. And then the gentleness would fade, replaced by an urgent passion....

But every time her thoughts strayed in that direction, she forced herself to remember the vow she'd made when she first moved to Cooper's Corner. She'd come to this town to lead a safe, quiet existence, and she would do nothing to disrupt anyone's life here. Which meant, of course, that she could never start a relationship. There were too many unanswered questions about her life before the accident—

"Miss Young?"

The voice startled her so thoroughly from her thoughts that Beth jumped violently. "Keegan," she said breathlessly, putting a hand to her heart. "I didn't hear you come in."

"Sorry." He gave her a sheepish look. "I didn't mean to scare you."

"That's okay. I was just...daydreaming instead of working." Beth smiled, but the mere sight of the boy caused her heart to beat a little faster. He looked so much like his father, with that gorgeous dark chestnut hair and those beguiling green eyes fringed with thick black lashes.

Someday a girl's heart is going to melt every time you look at her, Beth thought wistfully. "What brings you here on this beautiful summer day?"

"I need to get a book for my summer reading assignment," he explained.

She smiled in approval. "I'm impressed. A lot of students wait until the day before school starts to worry about their summer reading assignments. You're getting a head start. I admire your dedication."

"Thanks."

"Do you have a list?"

"Yeah, but most of the books sound pretty lame. I guess I'll read *Fahrenheit 451,* but I can't remember who wrote it."

"Ray Bradbury," she responded. "It's a terrific book. You'll enjoy it." Odd how tidbits like that just popped into her head, Beth thought. Of course, a lot of her knowledge about books and authors had been acquired since she'd started working in the library. Georgia had taught her so much, but sometimes movie titles and song lyrics would come to her, also.

She didn't understand how that could be if the part of her brain that stored long-term memories had been damaged, but it gave her hope, even after all this time, that someday her memory might return.

"Let me see if I can help you locate it." She came around the counter, and Keegan followed her to the fiction section. She ran her finger along the *B*s until she located Bradbury, then pulled the book from the shelf. "We only have one copy. You're lucky you came in early." She handed him the book. "Is this all you need, or do you want to look for something else?"

"No, that's all," he assured her quickly.

He was dedicated, Beth thought in amusement, but not that dedicated.

They walked back to the counter, and he fished his library card from his pocket. Beth opened the book cover and removed the card from the flap. The tiny library still used the card and stamp method rather than a scanner, although there was a computer in the office with a dial-up Internet connection. The simplicity of the system had made it easy for Beth to step in and take charge after Georgia had retired. That and the fact that Georgia had trained her well.

Beth's assistant, Lisa Darnell, a college student who worked part-time and summers at the library, came out of the office just as Beth finished stamping the due date on the blue card and slipped it into the sleeve.

"I'm all finished shelving," she announced.

"Already?" Beth glanced over her shoulder. "You made short work of that."

Lisa walked up beside her. "There weren't that

many overnight returns. I guess people around here are too busy with other things in the summer. Okay if I go to lunch now?''

"Sure.'' Beth handed the book to Keegan, who couldn't seem to tear his gaze from Lisa.

She saw him and smiled. "Oh, hey, Keegan.''

"Hi.''

The girl bent to retrieve her purse from underneath the counter. "I'll be back by twelve-thirty. Do you want me to bring you a sandwich or something?''

"No, but thanks,'' Beth said, still watching Keegan in amusement. "It's such a pretty day, I think I'll go out. Maybe walk across the street to the café.''

"Okay. See you later.'' Lisa waggled her fingers over her shoulder as she headed for the door.

"Here you go,'' Beth said, sliding Keegan's library card across the counter to him. But he still wasn't paying her the slightest attention. His gaze was focused on the door through which Lisa had just disappeared.

"Keegan?''

He jumped, as badly startled as Beth had been earlier. His face turned a bright red. "Sorry.''

"No problem.'' She smiled. "Here's your card.''

"Thanks.'' He stuffed the card into his shorts pocket and tucked the book under his arm. Then, with a careless wave, he bolted for the door.

As Beth watched him hurry from the building out into the bright sunshine, she couldn't suppress a smile. Unless she missed her guess, his dedication to his school assignment hadn't brought him to the library this morning. Or on any of his other recent visits. There was a far greater attraction here than mere books.

Well, she could hardly blame him. Lisa was a very pretty girl, with her choppy blond bob and wide blue eyes. The fact that she was several years older, a college woman, would only add to her allure.

Should she say something to Clint? Beth wondered.

No way, she immediately decided. She could be wrong about Keegan's infatuation, and it wasn't any of her business, anyway.

Besides, anything that brought her more deeply into Clint Cooper's orbit probably wasn't a good idea.

CLINT SEATED HIMSELF at his drafting table later that morning to work on plans for the conversion of one of the outbuildings behind the B and B into a guest cottage. But instead, he found himself pulling out a set of house plans he'd been working on for months. He almost had the drawings fine-tuned to his satisfaction.

In keeping with the local architecture, he'd designed a modern version of an old two-story farmhouse he'd seen years ago in upstate New York, complete with a red barn and a stone mill powered by a rushing brook. Clint knew the perfect spot on which to build the house. It was just down the road from Twin Oaks—a beautiful, grassy hillock surrounded by hundred-year-old hardwoods, with a breathtaking view of both the valley and the distant mountains.

He'd bought the parcel of land shortly after he and Maureen had begun renovations on the inn, but he hadn't mentioned the purchase to her because he never really figured the house would get built. But that didn't stop him from working on the project every chance he got, and Clint knew he wasn't alone in his endeavor. There wasn't an architect alive who didn't have a set of secret plans for his own dream house tucked away somewhere.

His design would probably surprise some of his former colleagues, he thought. The house was neither elaborate nor particularly elegant, but the rooms were spacious and well proportioned, and there were plenty of covered porches and long windows from which to enjoy the beautiful scenery. He could picture himself coming home to that place after a hard day's work. Keegan would be with him, the two of them anticipating the homey smells and the feminine smile that would greet them inside.

In Clint's fantasy, a woman watched for them at the window, but it wasn't Kristin's face he saw behind the glass. It was Beth Young's.

Which wasn't a good sign, he decided. Not that he was going to deny his attraction to Beth. He'd been drawn to her for months now, and after last night, he could have sworn she was attracted to him, too. He'd been almost certain an invitation gleamed in those beautiful violet eyes, an invitation he'd been fully prepared to accept. But there'd been something else in her eyes, too. A remoteness. A wariness. A warning that said *Don't get too close.*

Clint was too old for games. Too old to make a fool of himself over a woman who wasn't really interested. And besides, there was something about Beth that didn't quite ring true. He couldn't put his finger on it, but it was enough to make *him* wary. He'd been married to a woman who kept secrets from him, and Clint wasn't about to go down that road again.

The office door opened and Maureen walked in, looking like something one of their cats had dragged up.

Her hair was pulled back into a ponytail, but strands escaped and hung limply around her face. She had what appeared to be cookie dough or Silly Putty matted in her bangs, and there was a streak of something across her Twin Oaks T-shirt that Clint couldn't—and didn't want to—identify.

She walked across the room and plopped down behind the desk with a long, weary sigh.

He lifted a brow. "Rough morning?"

She rolled her eyes. "Don't ask. Do you know what the twins have already been into this morning?" Before Clint could answer, she put up a hand. "Don't bother guessing. You couldn't in a million years."

"Anything I can do?" he offered tentatively.

She glanced up. "As a matter of fact, there is."

Clint winced. He recognized the look on his sister's face. It said, *Yes, absolutely, there's something you can do, but you aren't going to like it.* "Well?" he ventured.

"I've been going over the bookings for this month. We're a little light toward the end of the month. Nothing to worry about," she hurried to assure him. "But I was thinking this might be a good time for each of us to try to get away for a few days. Don't say no immediately," she pleaded. "Just give it some thought. We've been working nonstop since we bought this place. First the renovations, then the grand opening, and now the expansion. Don't get me wrong.

I've loved every minute of it, and I absolutely think we did the right thing. The girls are thriving, and Keegan is, well, he's a different kid up here.''

"I agree."

"But I'm tired, Clint. I need a vacation."

"Then, by all means, take one."

"You don't think I'm being...frivolous?"

"Maureen, you've been putting in fourteen- and fifteen-hour days since we opened this place. If you think I'm going to accuse you of wimping out on me, I'm not."

She grinned. "I guess I was a little worried about that."

"Well, don't be. You may not still be a macho cop, but you're capable of holding up your end."

"I can still take you on," she declared.

"Still?" He gave a dry laugh. "Like you ever could, but dream on."

She eyed him speculatively. "I have to admit all that wood-chopping has given you some muscle tone, bro. You're looking pretty buff these days."

"Stop. I'm blushing."

"Of course, you still don't have *my* moves," she assured him.

He didn't bother to retort. "Have you run your vacation plans by Frank Quigg?" Quigg was Maureen's former superior in the NYPD and the man still in charge of the Nevil case.

"Not yet, but I will."

"Any idea where you want to go?"

Maureen shrugged. "The twins would love to go to Disney World, but that's out of the question. Quigg would never go for that."

"Probably not," Clint agreed.

"Besides, my checkbook's not up for Disney World, either."

"I could loan you the money."

"Clint, don't start."

"Maureen—"

She held up a hand. "Fifty-fifty, remember? I pull my own weight around here, financial and otherwise. That was the deal."

"It would just be a loan," he grumbled.

"You know what they say about loaning money to a family member."

"Yeah, the same thing they say about going into business with one."

She grinned. "Touché. But we haven't killed each other yet, so I call that a success."

"Oh, absolutely." Clint let the money matter drop, but it bothered him that Maureen wouldn't let him help her. She'd put her life savings into this inn, and Clint had matched her, cent for cent, but he hadn't taken the financial hit that his sister had. He'd drawn an impressive salary as an architect for a large firm in Manhattan. So impressive that some of his friends had thought him nuts for walking away. But Clint wondered what they'd say now if they could see Keegan. The happy, well-adjusted thirteen-year-old was a far cry from the sullen, smart-mouthed troublemaker they'd known in the city.

It pained Clint still to think about those days, how his son might have ended up.

"…so I was thinking we might just go to the beach for a few days. Build sand castles, tell jokes, sing silly songs. Just me and the girls."

"Sounds nice."

"They're growing up so fast," Maureen said with a misty smile.

"I know." Clint could sympathize. He was amazed every time he saw Keegan walk through the door these days. He was so tall and his voice had deepened over the winter. He was almost a man, Clint thought with a lump in his throat. Turning, he busied himself at his drawing board. "When did you want to go?"

"I thought you and I could sit down tonight and look at the calendar—" The phone rang, and Maureen picked up the receiver without finishing her thought. She listened for a moment, then nodded. "Yeah, he's right here. Hold on a sec." She handed the phone to Clint. "It's Keegan."

Problem? he mouthed.

She shook her head. *Don't think so.*

Clint lifted the phone to his ear. "Hey, what's up?"

"Hi, Dad. Nothing's up. I'm just, you know, hanging out." Keegan paused. "I thought maybe we could have lunch together."

"Well, sure," Clint said, trying to hide his surprise. "I guess I could rustle us up something—"

"I was hoping we could eat out."

"You want to ride out to the Burger Barn?"

"Uh, no. I thought we could eat in town. At the café."

"You want to eat at Tubb's Café?" He shot Maureen a glance, and she shrugged. "Since when?"

"I don't know, Dad. I just thought we could eat there. You know, just the two of us."

Okay, something was definitely up, Clint decided. Thirteen-year-old boys did not ask their fathers to lunch without ulterior motives. Especially not to Tubb's Café. "I guess I can get away from here for a while. How about we meet at one?"

"It has to be twelve-thirty!" Keegan insisted.

"Why twelve-thirty?" Clint glanced at his watch. "That barely gives me time to clean up and drive into town. One o'clock would be better for me."

"Yeah, but I, uh, can't do it at one. I, uh, promised Bryan I'd come over later. He and his mom are probably going back to Montana pretty soon."

Clint immediately relented. He knew Keegan had missed Bryan while he and his family had been at their ranch earlier that summer. If they were going back, it was only natural Keegan would want to spend time with his best friend. "Okay, I'll see you at twelve-thirty. You need me to pick you up from somewhere?"

"No, I'm at the…I'm already in town. I'll meet you at the café."

When Clint hung up the phone, he stared at the receiver for a moment, not sure what to make of the conversation.

"Anything wrong?" Maureen asked.

"Keegan just invited me to lunch."

"Hmm. You think he's trying to butter you up for something?"

"Could be," Clint mused. "But I have a feeling…"

"What?"

He shrugged. "I guess there's only one way to find out."

But he had the strangest feeling he was walking headlong into some kind of trap.

TUBB'S CAFÉ WAS on Main Street and drew a brisk lunchtime crowd through the week. The place was hopping by the time Clint got there right at twelve-thirty, but Keegan had managed to snag a booth near the windows. He was seated facing the door, and waved when Clint came in.

Clint walked over and slid into the booth across from his son. "Hey, buddy."

"Hi, Dad."

Clint glanced around. "Looks like Lori and Burt are really doing a good business today. Not an empty table in the place. You were lucky to get us a seat."

"I got here early," Keegan confessed.

"So what's the special occasion?" Clint regarded his son curiously.

Keegan was all innocence. "What do you mean?"

"I mean, it's not every day you call me up out of the blue and ask me to lunch. Something you want to talk to me about?"

"Not really."

"You sure?"

Color dotted Keegan's tanned cheeks. "I just thought it would be nice to have lunch away from home for a change."

When Keegan's gaze shot to the front door, Clint glanced over his shoulder. "You expecting someone else?"

Keegan shrugged. "No. I just, uh, thought I saw someone."

Okay, Clint thought. Something was definitely up with this kid. Not only had his lunch invitation been out of the ordinary, but he was acting suspicious as hell. His gaze kept darting to the front door, as if he were, indeed, expecting someone else, and he couldn't seem to make eye contact with Clint.

"Maybe you'd better tell me what's going on—" Clint broke off when the waitress brought over menus and tall glasses of ice water.

"Hello, Keegan. Mr. Cooper," the girl said in greeting.

Clint glanced up and smiled. "Hello, Trudi. How are you?"

"I'm fine, thanks." Tucking a strand of limp hair behind her ear, she gave him a wan smile. She was only eighteen, but there was a weary brittleness in her features, a sadness in her eyes that the smile couldn't reach. Trudi Karr was one of those eternally vulnerable people who couldn't seem to catch a break.

"What can I get you to drink?" She glanced from Clint to Keegan.

It might have been Clint's imagination, but he could have sworn the blush on his son's face deepened when the girl's gaze fell on him.

"Iced tea," Clint said.

"Coke," Keegan mumbled, not looking at Trudi at all now, but staring somewhere over Clint's shoulder.

Hmm, Clint thought, studying his son as Trudi turned and walked away. Was Trudi the reason for Keegan's sudden eagerness to dine at Tubb's Café? After all, he was thirteen. It wasn't unusual for a boy his age to get a crush on an older girl.

"Hey, it's Miss Young," Keegan said, as if sensing the direction of his dad's thoughts and wanting to head him off. He nodded toward the front of the café.

Clint whirled so fast he almost knocked over his water glass. Mopping at the splashes with his napkin, he turned just in time to see Beth walk through the door. And his heart almost stopped. Literally. He felt his chest tighten and his breath quicken. He couldn't take his eyes off her.

She looked as lovely as always in a slim dark skirt and a white, sleeveless top. She was a tall woman, and the hemline of her skirt, four or five inches above her knees, emphasized her long, slender legs. Her hair was pulled back and fastened at the nape. Clint preferred it loose and flowing over her shoulders, but this way was good, too, because he could fantasize about removing the clip, watching her slowly shake out those long, glossy curls....

The white streak at her widow's peak, so pronounced against the dark cloud framing her face, could have made her look gothic and uncanny, but instead it made her look...exotic.

And those violet eyes—

"*Dad?* Did you hear me?"

He turned back to Keegan. "What?"

Keegan gave him an odd, measuring look. "I said, all the tables are still full. Maybe we should ask her to sit with us."

Clint stared at his son in surprise. "You want her to join us for lunch?"

"I wouldn't mind," he murmured, glancing away.

Suddenly, it all became crystal clear to Clint, the reason his son had asked him to lunch. The reason he'd been so adamant about Tubb's Café at twelve-thirty. Keegan hadn't wanted to come here because of the food or Trudi Karr or even to spend time with Clint. On the contrary, Clint was nothing more than a cover. No, Keegan had wanted to come here at this exact time because somehow he'd known Beth would be here.

Clint's gaze narrowed on his son. It all made perfect sense now. Keegan's strange behavior. His secretiveness. His uncharacteristic trips to the library. His spying on Beth last night.

He had a crush on her.

His son had a crush on the same woman Clint himself was more than mildly attracted to.

He groaned inwardly. This was the stuff of a very bad soap opera, and unless he handled the situation carefully, with kid gloves, Keegan could get hurt and humiliated. Clint wouldn't be the cause of that for anything in the world.

Not even for a woman like Beth Young.

"So...are you going to ask her to sit with us?" Keegan persisted.

Clint said carefully, "Why don't you go ask her?"

"*Me?*"

"It was your idea."

"I know, but..." Keegan's expression was imploring. "I'm just a kid. It'd be better if you did it."

"You really want her to join us?" Clint prodded gently.

Keegan shrugged. "Sure. Why not? There's no place else for her to sit."

"Okay. If that's what you want." Clint got up and headed toward the front of the café where Beth still stood waiting for a table. As he approached her, he told himself he could handle the situation, no problem. After all, boys got crushes on older women all the time. It was no big deal. He'd been infatuated with his ninth grade English teacher. In fact, his feelings for her had been so strong that he could still remember the way his heart pounded every time Miss Stiles had walked into the classroom. She'd seemed so much older than him at the time, so much more worldly and sophisticated, but looking back, Clint realized she'd probably been only twenty-five or so. She was a real knockout, with long dark hair, big brown eyes and a body that had fueled more than a few forbidden fantasies.

Remembering all that now, Clint wondered if he should say something to Beth, warn her about Keegan's feelings, and maybe they could both figure out a way to let him down easily. But he couldn't broach the subject now. He'd have to wait until they were alone.

Although, Clint thought, noting the way her skirt softly molded to her slim hips, maybe being alone with Beth wasn't such a good idea, either.

He called her name, and when she turned, he could have sworn—hoped?—that the fleeting look in her eyes was pleasure.

"Clint, hi. I didn't expect to see you here."

"Keegan and I are having lunch." He glanced around the crowded café. "Looks like everyone decided to eat out today."

She nodded ruefully. "I should have come earlier or later."

"Or," Clint said, "you could join Keegan and me at our table."

Her brows lifted in surprise. "Oh, I wouldn't want to impose."

"You wouldn't be imposing. We're inviting you."

"But…" She glanced past him to Keegan. "I'm sure Keegan would like to have you all to himself."

"It was his idea."

"It was?" She looked pleased. "I don't know…"

"Come on. We insist." He stepped aside so she could precede him to the table.

"Well…if you're sure…"

"Absolutely."

Clint followed her back to their booth, and he couldn't help but notice the way Keegan scooted to the very edge of the bench, so that no one could sit beside him. Clint didn't quite know what to make of that. Maybe his son was too shy and nervous to have Beth sit beside him, and under the circumstances, Clint didn't feel he should say or do anything to draw attention to Keegan's actions. Without a word, he slid into the seat beside Beth.

The bench was wide enough to accommodate two adults comfortably, but Clint was acutely aware of her nearness. He was careful not to touch her, even accidentally, but he could smell her perfume—or was that her shampoo?—and the subtle scent was like a tantalizing whisper of seduction.

"Well, Keegan," she said with a smile. "It seems the two of us are destined to keep running into one another today."

Keegan glanced quickly at his dad, then averted his eyes. "Yeah, I guess so."

Beth turned to Clint. "Keegan came into the library this morning to check out a book for his summer reading assignment."

Clint looked at his son. Summer reading assignment? That was the first he'd heard about it. "Oh, really? And what book are you reading?"

Keegan shrugged. "I forget."

"You forget?"

"Fahrenheit 451," Beth interjected quickly. "I think he'll really enjoy it."

"Yeah, Bradbury's great," Clint agreed.

"You like Ray Bradbury?" Beth asked.

Clint grinned. "You sound surprised."

"No, it's just..." She paused, smiling. She had the most wonderful smile, he thought. Like moonlight on water. Soft, mysterious, fleeting. "I thought you were into Tom Clancy."

"I'm a man of wide and varied tastes," he assured her.

He saw her blush slightly, and Clint realized with a start that the two of them had slipped into a very subtle flirtation. It had happened so innocently and so naturally that he hadn't even noticed until it was too late.

Quickly, he scanned his son's face to see if Keegan had picked up on the vibes, but he seemed oblivious to the conversation. He seemed oblivious to everything but Beth. His gaze was fixed on her, and there was a strangely speculative gleam in his eyes.

A gleam that made Clint remember some of those fantasies he'd spun in class about Miss Stiles. A gleam that made him think it might be long past time for a heart-to-heart with his son.

Right now, however, he had to somehow extricate them all from a situation that could become very awkward, very fast.

Clint cleared his throat. "Maybe we should go ahead and order. I really need to get back to work."

He didn't look at Beth, but he sensed her stiffen slightly, as if he'd somehow offended her. That hadn't been his intent, of course, but neither did he want to hurt his son. If Keegan did have a crush on Beth...

Clint studied the menu almost furiously. Of all the women for his son to become infatuated with.

Of all the women for Clint to become attracted to.

And the hell of it was, she wasn't either of their types.

CHAPTER SIX

"SO HOW'D IT GO?" Bryan asked Keegan a little while later when they met at their favorite skating place—the pavement in front of an old abandoned gas station off Church Street.

Keegan shrugged. "Okay, I guess." He eyed the rickety ramp they'd rigged up with plywood and bricks. "Hey, check this out." He gathered speed as he skated toward the ramp, then at the top, he caught air and executed a perfect three-sixty, landed it easily, then glided back to Bryan.

"Not bad," Bryan said. "So what did your dad and Miss Young talk about?"

Keegan bent and checked the fastener on one of his skates. "Books mostly."

"Books?" Bryan made a face. "Why'd they talk about books?"

"I guess because Miss Young's a librarian."

"Yeah, but your dad is an architect. Buildings are a lot more interesting than books."

"Yeah." Keegan didn't really care what his dad and Miss Young talked about. He had other worries at the moment. "Now I've got to figure out a way to get him to ask her to dinner," he muttered.

Bryan skated around in a circle. "How're you going to do that?"

Keegan gave him a sidelong glance. "I've got an idea, but I'll need your help."

"No way." Bryan crossed his fingers in front of him, as if warding off something evil. All the while, he skated backward, away from Keegan. "You're not talking me into any more of your lame ideas. I don't want to get grounded for life."

"You won't get in any trouble."

"You always say that."

"Look, it's not for me, it's for my dad," Keegan cajoled. "Didn't you used to worry that your mom might get lonely and stuff before she got married again?"

Bryan shrugged. "I don't know."

Maybe that wasn't such a smart comparison, Keegan realized. He suddenly remembered that Bryan hadn't exactly been keen on the idea of his mom remarrying, and he hadn't liked Mr. McCabe at all in the beginning. But they were big buddies now. Mr. and Mrs. McCabe and Bryan and Bryan's little sister were all one big happy family. Was it so wrong for Keegan to want that, too?

"I just want my dad to be happy again," he said quietly.

Bryan heaved a resigned sigh. "All right, all right. What do you want me to do?"

Keegan grinned. "I thought you'd never ask. Here's the plan. We need to talk to your mom and convince her to call my dad—" When Bryan protested again, Keegan threw an arm over his shoulder. "Just be cool, okay? I'll do all the talking."

"That's what worries me," Bryan muttered, slinging off Keegan's arm.

"YOU'RE THROWING your dad a surprise party? Why, Keegan! That's the sweetest thing I ever heard," Bryan's mom gushed as she beamed at the two boys standing in front of her desk.

Bryan and Keegan exchanged glances. "Well, it's not really a party," Keegan explained. "It's just for family."

"Oh, I understand." She tucked a strand of brown hair behind one ear. "Tell me how I can help."

"I need to get my dad to the restaurant without him suspecting anything. I thought maybe you could call and tell him you want to talk to him about some new sets for the Christmas pageant or something." As the town's tourism director, Bryan's mom was in charge of the annual Christmas Festival and always came up with the coolest themes.

She looked at the boys doubtfully. "You think he'd buy that?"

"You could talk him into it, Mom. You know you could," Bryan urged. "Tuck says you could talk a dying man out of his last breath."

"Yes, well, Tuck says a lot of outrageous things," she grumbled, but her brown eyes sparkled with amusement. "Keegan, why don't you just have your aunt Maureen come up with some excuse?"

"Because he'd get suspicious," Keegan said. "And besides, she's not very good at keeping secrets."

"I see. Hmm. Let me think for a minute." Mrs. McCabe idly strummed her fingertips against the surface of her desk. "I suppose it might work if I told him the plans I had in mind were a bit complicated and I wanted to make sure they were structurally sound. You know, rely on his architectural expertise. Men love that,'' she murmured. Then, catching herself, she glanced at Keegan. "What restaurant did you have in mind?"

"The Blue Lantern Inn in Williamstown."

She lifted a brow. "That's a pretty fancy place, Keegan. Kind of romantic for a family gathering."

"It's my dad's favorite restaurant," Keegan said quickly, although he had no idea whether his dad had ever even been there. But the Blue Lantern was where a bunch of the seniors from his school had gone after the prom, so he figured it had to be pretty cool.

"The Blue Lantern it is, then," Mrs. McCabe said with a smile. She folded her hands and put them to her heart. "I just think this is so sweet, what you're doing for your dad. He'll be so touched. I didn't even know Clint had a birthday coming up."

Again, Keegan and Bryan exchanged quick glances, but luckily the phone rang, and Mrs. McCabe didn't seem to notice their uneasiness. When she hung up, she seemed a little frazzled herself. "Okay," she said briskly. "Let me jot all this down, and then I have to get back to work. The Blue Lantern Inn. Thursday night. What time?"

"Uh, seven-thirty."

"Seven-thirty. Got it." She looked up and smiled. "Okay, boys. I'll see what I can do."

"Thanks, Mrs. McCabe."

"Thanks, Mom."

"No problem. I'm glad to help. Now you boys scram and try to have some fun this afternoon. You've done your good deed for the day."

"GEE, I DON'T KNOW, Grace," Clint said evasively. The call from Grace McCabe had caught him completely off guard. He hadn't been able to come up with an excuse fast enough to get out of the favor she was asking. "I'm pretty busy around here with the new renovations and all."

"I'm not asking you to design anything," Grace explained. "I just want you to look over my plans and see if you can spot any potential problems. I wouldn't want anyone to get hurt. Remember last year when one of the horses bolted and the carriage my little Susan and I were riding in overturned? With all those people out for the parade, it's a wonder no one was killed." Grace paused, and Clint could picture her delicate shudder. "I don't want anything like that to happen again."

It *had* been a close call, Clint remembered. Too close, and he still wasn't convinced that Owen Nevil hadn't somehow been behind it. Maybe it would be a good idea for him to check out Grace's plans. "Okay," he said, thumbing through his calendar. "When did you want to meet?"

"I'm taking a few people to dinner tomorrow night at the Blue Lantern Inn in Williamstown to discuss all the plans I've made so far. Can you make it?"

"The Blue Lantern Inn?" he said skeptically. "That's a pretty ritzy place to hold a business meeting, isn't it?" And a long way to drive. Clint would have preferred something local.

But Grace airily dismissed the inconvenience. "I know it may seem a bit unusual, but that's the whole idea—to get people thinking outside the box. You know what I mean?"

"Uh, sure." Clint didn't have a clue what she meant. "I guess I'll see you tomorrow night then."

"Great. Thanks, Clint. I knew I could count on you."

"BUT I DON'T KNOW anything about putting together the Christmas Festival," Beth protested. "Your mother always does such a wonderful job, Bryan. Why in the world would she want my help?"

Before Bryan could answer her, Keegan spoke up. "She said she wanted your help with the music. Isn't that right, Bryan?" When Bryan didn't say anything, Keegan nudged him.

"Uh, yeah, that's right," Bryan agreed, giving Keegan a dark look. "She wants your help with the music."

"The note says she wants me to meet her tomorrow night to discuss it."

"At the Blue Lantern Inn in Williamstown," Keegan stressed. "At seven-thirty sharp." When Beth glanced up, he shrugged. "That's what she told us, anyway."

The note was typewritten on Grace's professional stationery. All the particulars were there, but something about the wording struck Beth as a little odd. "Maybe I should just give her a call to confirm—"

"No!" the boys said in unison.

"She's not there," Bryan said quickly.

"She had to go out of town," Keegan added.

"Out of town?" Beth asked with a frown. "When will she be back?"

"Tomorrow morning," Bryan said.

"Tomorrow night," Keegan said at the same time.

They exchanged looks. "Sometime tomorrow," Keegan clarified. "Before the meeting, but we don't know the exact time. Right, Bryan?"

"That's right."

"So it probably wouldn't do any good to call her."

"I suppose not." Beth glanced at the note again. What was it that was bothering her? She couldn't put her finger on it.

Oh, well. It sounded harmless, and it might even be fun. She didn't get out much, and a dinner meeting should be safe enough. As far as she knew, Clint wasn't on any of Grace's committees, so there'd be little chance of running into him, and that was a good thing, considering how awkward lunch had been earlier.

It had started out pleasantly enough, but then something had changed. There'd been subtle undercurrents that Beth hadn't understood. And as the meal progressed, Clint had grown more and more subdued, as if he couldn't wait to get away from her.

But he'd been the one to invite her to join him and Keegan. If he hadn't wanted her around, why would he have done that?

You're just being sensitive, Beth chided herself. And besides, what did it matter, anyway? Clint Cooper was off-limits, and the sooner she stopped thinking about him, the better off she'd be.

MAUREEN WHISTLED when Clint walked into the gathering room on Thursday evening. "Wow! Don't you look nice." She eyed him approvingly.

He tugged at his tie. "I feel like an idiot. I haven't worn one of these things since we moved to Cooper's

Corner. I don't know why Grace had to pick such a fancy place to hold a business meeting. I could just as easily have gone over her plans right here at the inn.''

"Oh, stop grumbling.'' Maureen batted his hand away from his tie and straightened it herself. "It'll do you good to have an evening out.''

"This isn't social,'' he was quick to remind her.

"I know, but there's no law says you can't enjoy yourself, is there?'' Maureen finished with his tie and stepped back to admire her handiwork. "I wonder why Grace didn't say anything about the meeting to me.''

"I have no idea, but you can go in my place if it means that much to you.''

Maureen gave him a dry smile. "Nice try, but you're the architect, so stop complaining and go render your expert opinion.'' She paused, her expression turning all innocent. "Will Beth be there?''

Clint frowned. "Beth? Why would she be there?''

Maureen studied her nails. "I just thought she might be the reason for the sport coat and the new pants.''

"I didn't want to look like some kind of hick,'' he muttered defensively.

"So, you don't know if Beth's going to be there or not?''

He sighed. "What difference does it make?''

"I just thought it might be a good time to ask her out, that's all.''

Clint shoved his hands into his pockets. "I'm not going to ask her out.''

Maureen glanced up with a frown. "You mean, you're not going to ask her out tonight."

"I'm not going to ask her out, period."

"Why on earth not?" Maureen's frown deepened. "What happened?" she asked almost accusingly.

Clint shrugged. "Nothing happened. I'm just not interested, that's all."

"Since when?"

"Maureen…"

Her features took on a stubborn resolve. "Don't you 'Maureen' me, Clint Cooper. You're the one being thickheaded about this. It'd be different if I thought you really weren't interested, but I know you are. I can see it every time you look at her, and don't even try to deny it."

"Okay, maybe I am a little attracted to her," he conceded. "But don't you think there's something kind of strange about her?"

"Oh, for crying out loud." Maureen threw up her hands in exasperation. "What are you talking about?"

Clint shrugged again. "What do we really know about her? What does anyone in town know about her? Where did she grow up? Where did she go to school? Why did she come to Cooper's Corner in the first place? She doesn't have family here. Why *here?*"

His sister looked as if she could cheerfully throttle him. "You know what? You're more suspicious than any cop I know. If we don't know that much about Beth, maybe it's because we haven't taken the time to ask. Besides," she added in a superior tone, "I *do* know something about her. Phyllis told me once that

Beth's grandmother and Georgia Cordell were childhood friends.''

"Georgia Cordell?'' Miss Georgia had been the town librarian for as long as anyone could remember until her retirement, when she'd handed the reins over to Beth. "Beth came to town because of Miss Georgia?''

Maureen nodded. "She came to tell Miss Georgia that her grandmother had died, and for some reason Beth decided to stay on. Miss Georgia got her a job at the library and pretty much trained Beth to be her replacement.''

"Just like that?'' Clint asked skeptically. "She pulled up roots, left her family and friends behind, a career—''

His sister rolled her eyes. "You don't know that. Maybe she was orphaned after her grandmother died. Besides, you and I did the same thing, Clint. We gave up our jobs, our friends, homes, everything to move here.''

"That's different. We lived here as kids, and we still have family here. Not to mention an inheritance.'' He waved a hand, encompassing the house.

"Yes,'' Maureen said quietly. "But the real reason we moved here was because we were both running away from something. Why are you condemning Beth for doing what you and I did?''

"I'm not condemning her,'' Clint said impatiently.

"Well, it sure sounds that way to me. It sounds to me as if you're making every lame excuse you can think of not to ask her out. You want to know what I think?''

"No, but I'm sure you'll tell me anyway," he said morosely.

Maureen's keen gaze narrowed on him. "I think you're afraid to ask her out because you're afraid you'll fall in love with her."

Clint's heart knocked against his chest. He wanted to deny his sister's accusation, but for some reason, he felt momentarily blindsided by it.

"Well?" she demanded.

He finally found his voice. "Drop it, Maureen. It's not going to happen. You're wasting your breath."

"How do you know it's not going to happen unless you—"

"Because Keegan has a crush on her, okay? Are you satisfied?"

Maureen's mouth dropped open. "Keegan has a crush on Beth Young? He told you that?"

"He didn't have to tell me. It's obvious." Clint ran a hand through his hair. "While we were at the café today, Beth came in. I had the distinct impression Keegan somehow knew she was going to be there. He insisted I invite her to join us. Then there was all that business last night about him spying on her. And Beth told me herself Keegan has been coming into the library a couple of times a week. Does that sound like the Keegan we know?"

"No, it doesn't," Maureen admitted. "But...you think it's because he's infatuated with Beth?"

"What else could it be?"

His sister's green eyes sparkled with sudden merriment. "Oh, Clint," she said, shaking her head. "Sometimes you really can be so clueless."

IN SPITE OF ALL the grumbling he'd done earlier, Clint actually enjoyed the drive to Williamstown. He headed north on Route 7, and the scenery was spectacular. Thick forests of hardwoods curved along the foothills, casting long shadows into the valleys and meadows. Where the woods thinned, pine trees sprouted, their feathery branches pungent in the coming twilight and burnished golden by the fading sunset. In the distance, the gentle slopes of the Berkshire Mountains glowed saffron against an ever deepening horizon.

It was the kind of evening that seemed full of promise and mystery, and for a while, Clint had the road to himself. He enjoyed the unusual solitude. The area was rural, but one was never far from civilization. The winter months drew hordes of recreational skiers to the mountains, and in the autumn, leaf-peepers flocked to the Berkshires in droves. The summer months attracted a different kind of tourist—couples mainly, who liked to picnic in the foothills and take leisurely strolls through the antique and specialty shops that lined the main streets of dozens of small towns.

Five years ago, Clint could not have imagined himself leading the kind of life he now enjoyed. He'd always secretly dreamed of living in the country, but he'd never thought he'd actually do it. Kristin had thrived in the city. She would have withered away in a place like Cooper's Corner.

Clint frowned, thinking about his late wife. If she hadn't died so suddenly, would they have lasted? Or had their marriage been over long before either of them was willing to acknowledge the fact?

Even though they'd married young, they'd once seemed so perfect for each other, and their hectic New York lifestyle had suited them both. They'd both been ambitious and loved to entertain, and Clint had a flair for cooking. He'd whip up gourmet meals while Kristin played the charming, accommodating hostess. Every Friday night, their apartment overflowed with clients and colleagues and friends.

And then after their guests had gone home, and Keegan was settled in bed, Clint and Kristin would retire to their own bedroom, where her penchant for adventure and risk-taking carried over into her love-making.

Clint had adored that about her at first. Loved the utter abandon with which she lived life and made love. He'd reveled in the fact that she couldn't seem to get enough of him.

But then came the realization that she couldn't get enough of him because he wasn't enough for her. Nothing was ever enough. Not a successful career. Not a loving husband. Not even an adoring son. She needed more. Craved more.

With that knowledge had come the dawning of Clint's own discontent. He'd tried to deny it until the very end, because he couldn't remember a time when he hadn't loved Kristin. It was what he did. Who he was. How could it be over?

Even on their last day together, he'd still been trying to make it work. He'd come home early to say goodbye because she was going to Boston for a gallery opening that weekend.

She was packing when he got home, and he came up behind her, slipping an arm around her waist and nuzzling her neck. To his surprise, she turned in his arms and pressed herself against him, kissing him in a way she hadn't kissed him in years.

"Wow," he said, pulling back. "What was that for?"

She smiled—almost sadly, he'd reflected later. "I'll miss you, Clint. You and Keegan."

"You'll be back on Sunday."

She didn't respond, but instead went back to her packing. When she finished, Clint carried her suitcase downstairs and saw her into a cab. She turned as the car drove away and waved to him through the back window.

As if she were never going to see him again.

The police had come to the apartment shortly after midnight to inform him that his wife had been in a terrible automobile accident. She'd been pronounced dead on arrival at the hospital, and her companion was in critical condition, not expected to make it through the night.

Her companion...

The questions had raged through him almost immediately, but Clint had shoved them aside while he tried to deal with the initial stages of shock and grief. There was so much to do. He had to find a way to tell Keegan. Make arrangements...

After the funeral, though, the terrible questions had come storming back. He'd started probing and had found out that Kristin's companion that night was an artist she'd discovered at a small gallery in SoHo. The two of them were having an affair. They'd even rented a loft together. She'd been planning to leave Clint for weeks.

For a while, bitterness and anger had overshadowed his grief. His ego reeled from the devastating blow, and the only way he'd known to overcome it was by throwing himself into his work, by keeping so busy during his waking hours that he didn't have time to think about his wife's betrayal. Her lies and secrets...

And then one day, while his cab was stuck in traffic, Clint had idly observed a group of kids on the street as they harassed the pedestrians who had the misfortune to walk by them. The thugs were all dressed alike: baggy jeans, oversize hooded sweatshirts, beanies pulled low over their ears. They wore similar colors, too. Gang colors. And their sullen, defiant expressions were nearly identical. It was hard to tell one from the other until the smallest kid turned toward the street, and Clint was shocked to recognize his own son. Keegan, only eleven years old, hanging out with a street gang.

It had been as devastating a blow as Kristin's betrayal, only this time it wasn't too late to make things right. Clint could still do something about his son, and when the opportunity presented itself, he wasted no time in getting Keegan out of the city. To his surprise, Keegan didn't put up a fight. He hardly argued at all. It was as if he'd been waiting for Clint to wake up from his stupor and rescue him.

Maureen had been right earlier, Clint thought grimly. He hadn't moved to Cooper's Corner because of their inheritance or their roots or because it had been his lifelong dream. He'd left the city because he'd been running scared, and Cooper's Corner had provided the sanctuary he and Keegan had both needed. Maybe Beth needed that sanctuary, too.

His scowl deepened as he watched the road. Why did everything always come back to Beth? Why couldn't he get her out of his head? He *needed* to get her out of his head, because it just wasn't going to work. Even apart from his son's crush, Clint couldn't shake the notion that there was something about Beth that wasn't quite right. A remoteness that made him very uneasy.

He'd been burned badly by Kristin's secrets and deceptions, and if he'd misjudged her so greatly—a woman he'd love his whole adult life—then how could he trust someone like Beth, a woman he knew nothing about?

Rely on your instincts, a little voice told him, but his instincts were warring with his hormones. The simple truth was he wanted Beth, more than he could remember wanting a woman for a very long time.

I think you're afraid to ask her out because you're afraid you'll fall in love with her.

His sister's earlier words came back to haunt him, and Clint said under his breath, "You're wrong, Maureen."

He was very much afraid he was already in love with Beth Young.

CHAPTER SEVEN

"THERE MUST BE some mistake."

"There's no mistake, sir. The reservation specifically requested a table for two on the terrace."

"And you're sure you've got the right name? Grace McCabe?"

Beth turned when she heard Clint's voice, and her heart almost stopped when she saw him. He looked so handsome, all dressed up. So tall and...manly.

He was standing only a few feet from her, talking with the maître d'.

"Look, there has to have been a mix-up somewhere..." Clint trailed off in midsentence when he spotted her. His brows lifted in surprise. "Beth?"

She gave a breathy little laugh. "Hi. I didn't expect to see you here."

The maître d' followed him to her table. "I was supposed to meet Grace McCabe, but there seems to be some problem with the reservations." He glanced around the nearly deserted terrace. It was a mild summer evening, but a cool breeze rippled through the trees, stirring a distant wind chime and keeping most of the diners inside. The blue lanterns strung around the perimeter of the terrace swayed gently, sending shadows scurrying over the tables.

Beth shivered, pulling her sweater over her bare arms. "I was supposed to meet Grace here, also."

"Shall I leave you two to sort things out, sir?" the maître d' inquired diplomatically.

"I guess you'd better." Clint sat down across the table from Beth, still looking perplexed. "Grace called you about tonight, too?"

"She sent me a note," Beth explained. "She said she wanted my input on the music for this year's Christmas pageant."

"She said she wanted me to look over some set designs to make sure they were structurally sound. She was pretty insistent." Clint shrugged. "I can't imagine why she isn't here yet."

"Maybe she's still out of town," Beth suggested.

"Out of town?"

"According to the boys, she had to go out of town yesterday, but they said she'd be back today in time for the meeting tonight."

Clint frowned. "What boys?"

"Keegan and Bryan. They brought me Grace's note."

Clint looked intrigued for a moment, then a speculative expression slowly altered his features. "No," he said almost to himself. "He wouldn't."

"What?"

"Why, that devious little sh—" He broke off, glancing at her almost sheepishly.

"Am I missing something here?" she asked hesitantly.

His smile was rueful. "We both missed something. I think we've been had, Beth."

"What do you mean?"

"This is embarrassing," he muttered. Beth couldn't see his face clearly in the candlelight, but she could have sworn he actually blushed.

"What's going on?" she asked in confusion.

He glanced up. "Unless I miss my guess, Grace McCabe was never going to show up here tonight. There never was a meeting."

"I don't understand," Beth said helplessly.

Shadows played across Clint's features, making him look even more handsome as he leaned toward her. "We're the victims of a diabolical scheme, Beth."

She caught her breath. "By whom?"

"My son."

"Keegan? But why would he do something like this?"

Clint winced. "I believe he's cooked up some kind of matchmaking plot."

"Oh. *Oh!*" Beth felt her face flood with color. She bit her lip. "Oh, dear." She could hardly meet Clint's gaze.

"Oh, dear, is right. To say this is awkward would be an understatement." He gave an apologetic shrug. "I knew he'd been acting a little strange lately, but I...well, I thought it was because he had a crush on you. Now I realize his intent all along was to get you and me together."

Beth's heart started to pound so hard she had to struggle to catch her breath. "Wh-what do you think we should do?" She glanced around, not knowing exactly where to look. If she looked at Clint... No, she couldn't look at Clint. She didn't dare look at Clint. "Should we...just leave?"

"We could," he said slowly. "And I could go home and throttle my son within an inch of his life. Or..." He paused, making Beth glance up at him. "We could have dinner together."

"You...still want to have dinner?" How could her heart beat so hard and not explode?

Clint smiled. "It seems a shame to drive all this way and not enjoy the ambiance."

"It is a beautiful restaurant." The blue lanterns seemed to float at the edge of the terrace, and where their glow dimmed, tiny white fairy lights had been entwined around tree limbs and climbing vines, creating a misty fantasyland effect. It was the perfect setting for romance. The perfect night, the perfect man...

"So you'll stay and have dinner with me?" Clint urged softly.

Her breath quickened at the way he looked at her, the way candlelight flickered in his eyes and across his face. "I'd love to."

He motioned for the waiter, and they both ordered a glass of wine, which came in cut crystal glasses that sparkled like diamonds in the candlelight.

Clint lifted his glass. "This place seems to call for a toast. What shall we drink to?"

Beth thought for a moment. "How about to Keegan?"

He laughed appreciatively. "To Keegan, who has no idea how much trouble he's in at the moment."

Beth sipped delicately, then set her glass aside. "I hope he's not in too much trouble. He really is a good kid, Clint."

"I know. And considering how far he's come—"

He broke off, setting his own glass down. "I hate to think what might have happened if we'd stayed in New York. He was headed for trouble, Beth. Serious trouble."

"His mother's death must have been devastating," she said. "For both of you."

Something hard glittered in Clint's eyes before he glanced away. "It was, in more ways than one." When she remained silent, his gaze returned to her. "My wife was an art critic, a very successful one. In fact, she was successful at anything she tried. She had this way about her. It's hard to explain." He stared into the darkness, a tiny frown pulling at his brow. "She was one of those…golden people."

Beth felt a stab of something that might have been envy. She wondered suddenly what Clint thought of her.

"I found out two days after her funeral that she'd been having an affair with an artist she'd discovered. They'd rented a loft and were planning to move in together. I never suspected a thing."

A wave of shock rolled over Beth. Clint's wife had planned to leave him for another man? How could that be? What kind of fool must she have been?

Clint toyed with his wineglass, looking uncomfortable. "I don't even know why I told you that. I've never told anyone. It was…a pretty big blow to my ego."

"I'm sorry." But what Beth really wanted to say was *Don't look so sad. The woman was obviously a fool.*

He studied his glass almost furiously. "For a while, I let my anger and bitterness consume me, and I didn't realize what it was doing to Keegan. I almost lost him.''

"But you didn't.''

"Thank God for second chances.'' He lifted his glass and took a sip of his wine. "So.'' His gaze deepened in the candlelight. "Now that you know all about my sordid past, do you still want to have dinner with me?''

She lifted her shoulders. "Why wouldn't I?''

He scowled. "A woman whose husband cheats on her is viewed as a victim in our society. A husband who has an unfaithful wife is usually called a fool. Or worse.''

Beth frowned. "I don't think you're a fool. You loved and trusted your wife.''

His gaze held hers for the longest moment. "Have you always had that knack?''

"Knack?''

"For knowing the right thing to say.''

It was Beth's turn to look away uncomfortably. "I...don't know.''

He seemed to sense her uneasiness. "Maybe we should go ahead and order.'' He picked up the menu and opened it. "What looks good to you?''

Beth wasn't the least bit hungry. She was too nervous, too aware of her attraction to Clint to think about food, but she went through the motions anyway, ordering the grilled swordfish at his suggestion, although she had no idea how she would get it down.

After the waiter quietly vanished, Clint leaned toward her. "It hardly seems fair, you know.''

She fiddled with her napkin. "What doesn't?''

"You know so much about me and yet I know hardly anything about you."

"There isn't much to tell," she said with a shrug, but her heart clamored inside her chest.

"I find that hard to believe." His gaze was deep and probing. Mesmerizing. "Cooper's Corner is a long way from California."

Not as far as she might have hoped, Beth thought, remembering the face in the window the other night at Twin Oaks. She shivered, as much from Clint's relentless gaze as the memory.

"What brought you to town, Beth?"

She took a deep breath and watched one of the lanterns as it rocked gently in the breeze. So this was it, she thought. The moment of truth. What should she tell him? *How much* should she tell him? "I came to Cooper's Corner to...recuperate."

"You were ill?"

"I was in an automobile accident two years ago. A serious one. In fact, I went into cardiac arrest. After my heart was resuscitated, I lapsed into a coma. When I woke up, I was told I'd sustained a serious head injury, among other things. I couldn't remember who I was or where I lived or...anything." She met his gaze finally, expecting to see shock and dismay, maybe even revulsion, but the emotion gleaming in his eyes seemed more like concern.

"You had amnesia?"

"Yes."

"Wow." He sat back in his chair. "That must have been frightening. How long did it take to get your memory back?"

"I never got it back."

"You mean—" Now came the shock.

Beth forced herself to hold his gaze. "I still don't know who I am. Or where I came from. Or what I did in my past. My life before the accident is a complete blank."

Clint ran a hand through his hair, obviously at a loss. "You don't remember *anything?*"

"No."

"But your name—"

"It was given to me by the woman I shared a room with in the hospital after I was moved from Intensive Care. Her name was Addie Young, and she had terminal leukemia. Her granddaughter, Beth, had drowned a few years earlier in Mexico, in a scuba diving accident while she was on spring break. Her body was never recovered, and Addie never petitioned the court to have her declared legally dead. I guess she held out hope for a long time...." Beth trailed off, realizing she was straying from the topic. "Anyway, Beth's—the real Beth's—parents were dead, and Addie had no one. She took me in when we were both released from the hospital because I had nowhere to go."

"What about your family?" Clint's voice still sounded shocked, subdued, as if he couldn't quite absorb everything she was telling him. "I mean, you didn't remember them, but they remembered you, right?"

Beth shook her head. "There was no one. The accident occurred on Big Bear Mountain in San Bernardino County. The police thought I might have gone there on vacation, and that's why no one had reported me missing and why no one in the area recognized me. But they never turned up anything in their investigation.''

Clint leaned toward her. "What about identification? A driver's license, credit cards. There must have been something."

"My car went over an embankment and plunged into a river. Somehow I swam out. I don't…remember how. A man who saw the accident called the paramedics and the rescue team. They barely got me out before a mudslide brought down part of the mountain. The car was buried.'' She shrugged, not wanting to take it any further.

The briefcase, the money, the gun…that explanation would come later if Clint still wanted anything to do with her after what she'd just told him. She would tell him that the police, after their first initial visit, had speculated as to why nothing from the car had survived but the briefcase, and that it seemed to them, in hindsight, that the briefcase might have purposely been thrown onto that mountain, rather than by accident, as they'd first thought. For what reason, they could only guess, but they hadn't been willing to dismiss their suspicions of her. They still weren't able to say, without a doubt, that they believed Beth to be innocent of any wrongdoing.

Yes, all that would come later if Clint still wanted to know more about her, but somehow Beth didn't think it would come to that. She was a woman who couldn't remember her past. If he wasn't discomforted by that fact for his own sake, he surely would be for his son's.

"So why did you come to Cooper's Corner?" he asked finally.

"Addie's family had a summer home there when she was a little girl. She remembered the town fondly, and she thought it would be a safe place for me to start a new life."

"Safe?"

"Peaceful."

Their gazes collided over the candle flame. Clint shook his head. "I don't know what to say. This is all so incredible."

"It's a lot to take in," Beth agreed. "And now that you know about me, do you still want to have dinner?"

"Of course." He smiled at her across the table, but there was something that might have been doubt flickering in his eyes.

IT WAS A RELIEF to Beth when dinner was finally over.

Not that she hadn't enjoyed her time with Clint. She had, perhaps a little too much. He'd gone out of his way to try and help her relax after her revelation, but Beth had known he was shocked. He must have had dozens of questions about her memory loss and her past, but he'd restrained himself admirably. He'd listened closely to everything she'd told him, but he hadn't pressed her for more.

Which was a good thing, because she wasn't ready to tell him about the money or the gun or the police's lingering suspicions. She wasn't ready to see the tiny flicker of doubt in his eyes turn into something darker and deeper. Something harder to conceal.

Oh, she would have to tell him at some point. She knew that. She'd seen how deeply wounded he'd been by his wife's secrets and deception, and Beth would never do that to him again. A relationship couldn't be based on half-truths and evasions. Love couldn't thrive on anything but total honesty—

She stopped herself short. Love? What made her think that she and Clint were going to fall in love? That they were embarking on a serious relationship?

He'd given her no indication that he had plans for a future with her. All he'd done was graciously ask her to stay and have dinner with him once his son's scheme had been unveiled. Beth suspected that, deep down, he'd been as anxious as she for the evening to end. He'd walked her to her car and then mumbled something about having to stop for gas. Beth had interpreted that as an excuse for why he couldn't follow her home. Actually, she was relieved. She would have been nervous if he'd been driving behind her all the way home. This way she had the road to herself, and she had plenty of time to think.

For all the good it did her.

Unfortunately, all the thinking in the world couldn't produce a conclusion other than the obvious. A relationship with Clint wouldn't work. Even if she were completely honest with him, even if he—and this was a very big if—could accept the possibility that she might have done something terrible in her previous life, it wouldn't work for one simple reason. They could never be sure her past wouldn't come back to haunt them. The uncertainty would be a dark cloud hanging over them always.

It was best that she end it now, before anyone got hurt, Beth decided as she pulled into her own driveway. And if she couldn't forget Clint, if she couldn't get over her feelings for him, then she might have to move away from Cooper's Corner. She hoped it wouldn't come to something so drastic, but she wouldn't be responsible for disrupting Clint's and Keegan's lives, nor would she ever knowingly put them in the path of someone who might be set on her destruction.

Hardening her resolve, Beth got out of the car and crossed the yard to her tiny porch. As she inserted the key into the lock on her front door, a car came speeding around the corner, catching her in the glare of headlights.

She blinked, her hand going automatically to shade her eyes. When the car pulled to the curb in front of her house, fear darted through her, but then almost immediately she recognized Clint behind the wheel.

She watched him get out of his car and stride up the walkway to her porch. He'd shed his coat and tie, and he looked very masculine standing at the bottom of the steps, gazing up at her. Moonlight slanted shadows across his features, making him seem dark and mysterious, but not frightening. Never frightening.

"I couldn't let it end that way," he said softly. "We didn't even say good-night."

"We did at the restaurant—"

"That wasn't a proper good-night." Slowly he climbed the steps, and when he reached the porch, he didn't say another word, but instead cupped her face in his hands and kissed her.

Beth closed her eyes, trying to steel her resolve, but the thrill of having his lips against hers was something she hadn't been prepared for. He kissed her gently at first, a soft, whispery caress, but even then there was an edge of desperation in the way his hands tangled in her hair, in the way he parted her lips with his. His tongue dipped inside her mouth, and something went all warm and still inside her.

He lifted his head, searching her face, and then finding what he wanted to see, he kissed her again. The gentleness was gone now, replaced by an urgent passion that stole her breath away. He wrapped his arms around her, pulling her close, pressing their bodies together until she could feel his heart beating against hers. Beth's arms slipped around his neck, and this time her lips parted of their own volition. This time it was her tongue that dipped inside.

She felt the immediate response of Clint's body as he groaned softly into her mouth. Her knees trembled at the knowledge that he was as deeply aroused as she.

When he drew away again, he rested his forehead against hers. "Wow," he said with a ragged breath.

Beth shuddered. "Is it always…do you always kiss like that?"

He laughed softly. "You inspire me."

His lips moved against her hair, and Beth sighed. "It's getting late. I should go in."

"I know. I have to get up early, too. We have a full house, and the guests will expect griddle cakes at the crack of dawn," he said ruefully.

"I've heard about your griddle cakes." Beth's fingers played with the buttons on his shirt. "They're something of a legend around here."

"I'll have to make them for you sometime." His voice deepened intimately, conjuring an image of breakfast in bed, with lots of whipped cream and warm maple syrup.

She felt her face color in the darkness. "I really should go in." She turned toward the door, but Clint tugged her back.

"Not quite yet," he murmured, dipping his head to kiss her again. He leaned against the wall, pulling her against him until she was nestled in his arms. A safe place to be, Beth thought fleetingly, until his kiss deepened, and she realized suddenly that she wasn't safe at all. She was in grave danger of losing her heart, and that couldn't happen. *They* couldn't happen. Someone would get hurt, and Beth was very much afraid she was already too late to stop it.

"Kiss me, Beth," he urged against her ear.

I can't, she wanted to tell him. *I shouldn't.*

But kiss him she did, with a heated recklessness that was as foreign to her as her past. She was like a different woman in Clint's arms, a woman who knew what she wanted and how to get it. A woman who was no stranger to romance, to love, to passion.

"This is getting dangerous," he whispered, when they broke apart. He laughed shakily. "Maybe I'd better go before..."

Before things get out of hand, Beth thought, but this time she was the one who pulled him back into her arms. The one who murmured against his mouth, "Not quite yet."

WHEN CLINT GOT HOME, he went straight to Keegan's room. Opening the door, he glanced inside. The light was off, but in the moonlight streaming in from the window, he could see his son's form beneath the covers. Keegan's back was to him, and he didn't stir at all when Clint called his name.

"Son? You awake?"

Still no response.

Clint started to back out of the room, but then he turned and said very quietly into the dark, "I just wanted you to know I had a nice time tonight. Thanks." Then he closed the door softly between them.

KEEGAN WAITED until his dad's footsteps had faded, then he pushed off the cover and swung his legs over the side of the bed. He was fully dressed. All he had to do was slip on his shoes.

Making quick work of that, he tiptoed across the room and unlatched the window. He'd used his skateboard wax on the frame a few days ago, and now the window lifted without a sound.

Hitching a leg over the sill, Keegan paused for a moment, listening to the night. All was quiet. The coast was clear. Only one more thing to do before his mission would be complete.

BETH AWOKE with a start, certain that someone was in her house. And that the intruder had come to kill her. But as she lay still for a moment, listening to the quiet darkness, she realized the muffled sound that had pulled her from sleep had been nothing more than her imagination, a remnant of the nightmare she'd had earlier.

Nothing to be afraid of. All was well.

She'd just made up her mind to try and get back to sleep when the noise came again, louder this time. Not from inside the house, she realized with a shiver, but from the front porch. Someone was trying to break in.

Heart pounding, she got up quietly and bent to retrieve the baseball bat she kept under her bed. Gripping the wood, she crept ghostlike down the hallway, checking all the doors and windows along the way. When she reached the living room, she paused, her gaze glued to the front door, watching and listening for a sign of the would-be intruder. A stealthy footfall on the porch, the rattle of the doorknob...

There was nothing.

Gathering up her courage, she crossed the darkened room and turned on the porch light, then drew back the gauzy curtain on the front door. Peering out into the night, she searched the porch and the shadows beyond, but again she saw nothing. She was just about to turn away when something drew her gaze to the yard.

Eyes gleamed in the darkness.

Beth caught her breath, but immediately released it with a shaky laugh. The glowing eyes belonged to her neighbor's cat. And the noise she'd heard was from a potted geranium he'd knocked over on her steps. Instead of running from the scene of the crime, he perched defiantly on her walkway.

As if to prove to herself there was nothing to be afraid of, Beth released the lock and drew back the door to peer cautiously out. "Dagwood," she scolded softly. "Shame on you! Look at that mess."

The cat eyed her balefully for a moment, then got up and stalked off into the night.

Beth watched the cat disappear into the darkness, and just as she was about to retreat back into the house, she paused as a familiar scent drifted on a stray breeze. Roses...

She glanced down. A single red rose lay on her doormat.

Her heart quickened. From Clint?

It didn't really seem like something he'd do. She couldn't imagine him sneaking around in the middle of the night to leave a rose on her doorstep, but whoever had done it hadn't bothered to remove the thorns from the stem. She picked it up carefully, lifting the blossom to her face. The velvety petals tickled her nose, and for a moment, she closed her eyes, drinking in the scent.

Then, all of a sudden, a blinding headache seized her. White-hot light exploded inside her head, and the rose fell to the floor as she grabbed her temples, trying to press away the pain.

Through the terrible throbbing, something came to her. Gunshots. Two of them. One after the other. Bam! Bam!

And then a scream.

When the pain subsided, Beth found herself trembling so badly she had to grab the door frame to steady herself. She stared down at the rose in disbelief. In horror.

Someone from her past had found her.

CHAPTER EIGHT

"WHAT DO YOU MEAN, she's not coming tonight?"

"She called and said she wasn't feeling well," Maureen said as she rushed past Clint into the gathering room. "That's all I know." She stopped suddenly to pluck a withered daisy from an arrangement on a rosewood table in the foyer, and Clint, who was following her, almost plowed into her.

"How did she sound?" he persisted. "Did she sound sick?"

Maureen spun in exasperation. "I didn't ask her for a blow-by-blow description of her symptoms, Clint. I'm sure she's fine. Now quit brooding and make yourself useful. We have enough to worry about trying to figure out how to entertain our guests tonight since Beth won't be playing."

"This isn't a cruise ship," he said dryly. "Our guests don't have to be entertained twenty-four hours a day. I'm sure they can manage on their own just fine for another evening without Beth. After all, that's why they come to a bed-and-breakfast. For the peace and quiet."

"Oh, thank you, Clint, that was ever so helpful." Maureen tossed the dead daisy into a nearby trash can, then gave him an irritable glance. "Look, you can either stand around here brooding all night or you can go call Beth and find out for yourself how she's doing. Or better yet, go see her in person.''

"If I didn't know better, I'd think you were trying to get rid of me," Clint muttered.

"You're no good to me in this state," his sister said bluntly.

"I'm just concerned that she might really be sick. She doesn't have anyone to look after her."

Maureen headed for the registration desk. "So, go. Be her hero."

"That's not what I'm trying to do—"

"Did I hear someone mention Beth Young?" a voice inquired behind them.

Maureen and Clint turned at the same time, and Clint stifled a groan. Their distant cousin Phyllis Cooper had come to the house earlier with her daughter, Bonnie, who'd been called out for an emergency plumbing repair in one of the upstairs bathrooms. Phyllis had obviously caught on to the end of Clint and Maureen's conversation, and now her gaze darted back and forth with avid curiosity.

"I was just telling Clint that she won't be playing tonight," Maureen said carefully.

"That's funny. She wasn't at the library today, either." Phyllis's brow wrinkled in consternation. "I wonder if she's sick."

"I'm sure she's fine," Clint muttered. The last thing Beth needed was to attract the attention of Phyllis and her husband, Philo. A nosier pair he couldn't imagine. Oh, he supposed they meant well. They were kind and gentle people, never deliberately spiteful with their gossip, but they could be relentless.

"Alton Darnell's daughter was working at the library," Phyllis was saying. "Lisa, I think her name is. Pretty little thing. Goes to State College. Anyway, she wasn't very helpful, I'm afraid, because she was more interested in batting her baby blues at Gerald Lowery's boy—you know, the one with all that scraggly hair?—than in helping me find my book. The kid was lurking in the reference section, as if no one would notice him, but for crying out loud, he stuck out like a sore thumb. He flunked out of high school, you know. He had to enroll in a trade school over in Pittsfield, and I know Louise, his poor mother, is just about at her wit's end—"

"Phyllis," Maureen gently interrupted. "Was there something you needed?"

Her brows drew together. "Well, yes, of course there was. Beth called yesterday and told me she had the new Mary Higgins Clark book put aside for me, so I stopped by today to check it out, and—"

"I mean, was there something you wanted from us?"

"Oh. Oh, that!" She gave a good-natured laugh. "It slipped my mind completely. Philo says I'd forget my head if it wasn't attached. Bonnie sent me down here to tell you she has the leak in the corner bathroom temporarily fixed, but she's going to need a doohickey she has to special order from someplace in New York to do the job properly. She says she'll have Jaron pick it up while he's in the city."

Bonnie was the town plumber and an expert in old—even ancient—fixtures. She knew more about antique ball cocks and pressure valves than any woman had a right to, and she'd saved Clint's hide from near disaster more times than he cared to remember on the occasions he'd embarked on a do-it-yourselfer. He could design anything, cook anything, was even a fair carpenter, he'd discovered. But he was a total washout as a plumber.

Thank God for Bonnie. She'd married last fall, but luckily for Twin Oaks and for Clint, she and her husband, Jaron Darke, had decided to split their time between Cooper's Corner and New York, where he was a columnist for one of the major papers. Also luckily for the inn, she was willing to come out at all hours.

This time, she'd brought Phyllis with her, although as far as Clint could see, the older woman hadn't been much help. She'd spent most of the evening in the gathering room, gossiping with her friends and pumping the guests for local news.

"Did Beth say why she can't play tonight?" Phyllis inquired delicately.

"She said she's not feeling well." Maureen shot Clint a warning glance.

"Is it the summer flu?" Phyllis seemed genuinely concerned. "That's going around, you know. Ethel Mayberry had it last week. The doctor gave her one of those new drugs that supposedly eases the symptoms, but for my money, it's hard to beat a bowl of chicken soup. That's what I always give Philo when he's under the weather."

When she finally paused for air, Maureen said quickly, "Will you excuse us, Phyllis? I've got a million things to do, and you were just on your way out, weren't you, Clint?"

"Uh, yeah." He snapped to the cue and gave his sister a grateful nod.

"Give Beth my regards," Phyllis called innocently, when he'd turned toward the door.

"I will—" He stopped short, realizing how easily he'd fallen into her trap. When he glanced back, Phyllis's eyes gleamed with triumph.

Clint stifled another groan. By tomorrow morning, it'd be all over town that he had a thing for Beth Young. By the end of the week, the local gossips would probably have them engaged.

He wondered why that prospect didn't bother him as it might have once.

BETH SAT ON HER SOFA and stared into the dark. Night had long since fallen, but she hadn't bothered to turn on a lamp in the living room. Light spilled out from the bedroom, however, throwing huge shadows across the walls and ceiling. The house seemed cold and eerie. Lonely, somehow.

From where she sat, she could see into her bedroom. Her suitcase was open on the bed and clothes were strewn over the spread. She'd packed and unpacked so many times that day she'd lost count. Her instinct for survival screamed for her to run, to hide, to protect herself from her past. Another part of her argued to stay and fight. Find out once and for all what she had to fear, *who* she had to fear. Because if she ran this time, Beth knew that it would never be over. She would never be able to stop running.

When her doorbell sounded, she jumped, her hand going to her throat as her head swiveled toward the door. Breath suspended, she watched and waited, expecting that any moment someone might come bursting in. But that was crazy, she chided herself. A killer wouldn't ring her doorbell. He'd creep in through an unlocked door. Slither in through an open window—

"Beth!"

Clint's voice. Her heart started to hammer. She couldn't tear her gaze from the door, but neither did she get up to answer it.

The bell sounded persistently, then he called out her name again. "Beth? Are you all right? Maureen said you were sick. We're all worried about you. Beth!"

She got up and crossed the room. Unfastening the lock, she drew back the door. Clint stood with one hand planted on the frame, staring down at her. She hadn't turned on the porch light, but in the illumination from the street, she could see that his eyes were dark, his expression drawn with worry.

"Are you okay?"

His voice was so deep. So full of concern. Something inside Beth started to melt. "Yes, I'm fine."

"You don't sound fine." Clint cocked his head. "Do you want me to call a doctor?"

"No, really, Clint. I'm fine. I'm just…a little under the weather."

His gaze seemed to intensify as he stared down at her. "Does this have anything to do with last night?"

At once she became acutely aware of where he stood. Right outside her front door, where he'd kissed her the night before. Where she'd kissed him back. Where she'd fallen in love—

No. Oh, no. She couldn't think that way. She couldn't be in love with Clint Cooper. She couldn't be in love with anyone. Not now. Not ever.

''Beth.'' He sounded so gentle she wanted to weep.
''What's wrong?''

''Nothing—'' But her voice broke, and Clint put
out a hand to touch her arm.

''This *is* about last night, isn't it?''

She shook her head. ''No. Not in the way you
mean.''

''In what way then?'' When she didn't reply, he
said almost urgently, ''Can I please come in?''

She knew she should say no, but she couldn't. She
simply couldn't. She stepped back to allow him to
enter, then closed the door behind him.

Flipping on a light, she turned to face him. He
gazed around, curious about where she lived. She
wondered what her home said about her. The furnish-
ings were sparse, but she liked to think elegant, and
the house itself had tons of character. It was a Crafts-
man-style cottage, built in the 1920s, with gleaming
hardwood floors and charming arched doorways.

The house was the only purchase she'd made with
the money Addie had left her. The amount of the
inheritance had astounded and troubled Beth when
she'd learned of it, and she'd given most of it away
to charity. She'd retained enough to start a new life
in Cooper's Corner, and now every month, instead of
making a payment to a mortgage company, she sent
a check to the Leukemia Foundation. It was the least
she could do for a woman who'd literally given her
a new life.

But now was not the time to dwell on all that.

Not when her past was literally nipping at her
heels.

She glanced hesitantly at Clint. "I'm really fine. You didn't have to come over."

He took a step toward her, but stopped when she moved back. "What's happened since last night?"

"Last night was a mistake."

He gave her an incredulous look. "You didn't really say that. That's such a cliché. Come on, Beth. Tell me the real reason you're so upset?"

She hesitated for a moment longer, then finally relented. Walking over to her desk, she picked up the wilting rose. "Someone left this on my doorstep last night."

His mouth tightened. "Are you trying to tell me there's someone else in your life?"

Beth was appalled that he'd jumped to that conclusion. "No. No! I don't know who left the rose."

He looked relieved. "A secret admirer?"

She shook her head.

"Well," he said, gazing at the rose. "Given the circumstances of our dinner last night, I suppose Keegan could have left it."

"It wasn't Keegan."

The certainty in her voice seemed to surprise him. "How do you know? He could have pilfered it from Maureen's garden."

"The rose was left on my porch after midnight. Keegan wouldn't have been out that late, would he? Not without your knowledge."

"I would hope not, but—"

"I think whoever left the rose was someone who knew it would upset me," Beth insisted.

"Why would you think that?"

"Because when I saw that rose last night, I...remembered something."

Clint's brows lifted. "Are you trying to tell me you got your memory back?"

"No, nothing like that. I'm not even sure it was a memory. It was more like a...vision. An impression. The rose meant something to me...." She shook her head helplessly. "I don't know how to explain it. But somehow I think it's associated with...violence. With gunshots and a scream..."

He took her arms and held her gently. "I'm completely lost here, Beth. I want to help you, but I'm afraid I don't have the slightest idea what you're talking about."

"I know you don't. How could you?" She pulled herself from his hold. "When I told you about the accident last night and my amnesia, I didn't tell you the whole story."

Something flickered in his eyes. "I'm listening."

"Maybe we'd better sit down," she murmured.

"I don't like the sound of that." But he followed her to the sofa, and they sat at opposite ends.

Beth folded her hands in her lap. "While I was still in the hospital, recuperating after the accident, the police came to see me."

"You told me that. You said they were trying to find out your identity."

She nodded. "Yes. But they were also trying to prove I'd done something wrong. Something...criminal."

He frowned. "What do you mean?"

She told him about the briefcase of money and the gun, about the police's suspicions and all the doubts she had herself. When she finished, she couldn't look at him. "If you want to go now, I'll understand. In fact, I think that's what you should do."

"Beth, look at me." When she finally glanced at him, his eyes gleamed with emotion. "I'm not a fair-weather friend. I don't bolt at the first sign of trouble."

Friend? Was that all they were? Friends? Beth felt something wither inside her. "I don't expect anything from you, Clint. Last night—"

"Last night wasn't a mistake, so don't even go there. I've wanted to kiss you for a long time. You have no idea...." Though his words trailed off, his eyes held a hint of something Beth didn't dare hope for.

She released a shaky breath. "Before we...before you come to any conclusions about me, there's something else you should know. There was an eyewitness on the mountain that night. He saw my car go over the side. He thought I might have been forced over."

"What?" Clint moved beside her on the sofa.

"Someone may have tried to kill me that night. I don't know for sure. But the police seemed to think it was possible. They were convinced it was all tied together somehow—the money in the briefcase, the gun, my being alone on a mountain road in the middle of a rainstorm. They think I was running from someone, or from something I'd done. Or both." She shook her head. "We just don't know."

Clint was silent for a moment. "I hardly know what to say."

"I can imagine."

"If someone did try to kill you that night..."

She nodded. He'd caught on fast.

"That's why you're so upset about the rose." He glanced at her worriedly. "You think whoever left it may want to harm you, don't you? You actually think you're in danger."

"No...maybe. I don't know for sure. But I guess I have to consider the possibility."

"But it doesn't make sense, Beth. Think about it. If someone wanted to hurt you, why didn't he just break into your house? Why let you know he's onto you?"

"To send me a message? To torment me?" She wrapped her arms around her middle. "I don't know. I just know...it's not safe for you to be here, to be around me. I want you to leave, Clint. I don't want to drag you into this."

He still looked incredulous at the whole story. "If you're really in danger, you can't expect me just to turn my back on you. I'd never do that. We have to get some help here. I'll call Scott Hunter. He's a friend of mine."

At the mention of the state trooper, Beth put her hand on his. "Please don't. Don't get involved, Clint. I'm serious. I can handle this."

"How?"

Her gaze strayed inadvertently to the bedroom door. Clint's gaze followed, and she heard him swear under his breath.

"Why is there a suitcase on your bed?" When she didn't answer, he took her arm, forcing her to face him. "Is that how you're going to handle it? By running away?"

"I've been running for two years," she said softly.

"I realize that now. I thought I had a home here, a new life, but I was only fooling myself. All I've been doing is biding my time until my past caught up with me. And now it has."

"So you're going to leave, just like that? After last night?" His eyes glittered with anger, but Beth forced herself not to back away. She had to finish this, here and now, because where she was going, she didn't want Clint following her.

"Forget last night. Pretend it was just a dream," she said harshly. "A beautiful, impossible dream."

WHEN CLINT GOT BACK to Twin Oaks, Maureen was alone in the kitchen, sipping a cup of coffee.

"Where is everyone?" he asked absently.

She shrugged. "The guests have gone up to their rooms, the twins are in bed and Keegan's on the computer, I think. All is well with the world. Although…" She gave him a long perusal. "Not with you, I see. Can I get you a cup of decaf?"

He nodded vaguely, and while Maureen poured his coffee, Clint pulled out a chair and sat down at the table. When she brought over the cup, he said hesitantly, "I need to talk to you about something. But it can't go any farther than this room. Unless…well, unless I give you the green light. Understood?"

Her gaze deepened with concern. "Clint, what is it?"

"You have to give me your word first. You're not a cop anymore. I want you to remember that. You don't have the kind of obligations you did when you were on the force."

"All right, but what on earth is the matter? You

look like death warmed over. What happened with Beth tonight?"

He let out a ragged breath. "It's a long story, I'm afraid."

Maureen settled more deeply into her chair. "I've got all night."

He took a drink of his coffee and winced.

"Sorry," she muttered. "I should have made a fresh pot."

"No, it's okay." Actually, the bitter aftertaste matched his mood, Clint decided. "Last night, when I got to the restaurant, Grace wasn't there. No one was there except Beth."

Maureen perked up. "Beth? What was she doing there?"

"I haven't had a chance to talk to Grace yet, but I'm guessing Keegan had her set the whole thing up, just so that Beth and I would have dinner together."

A smile tugged at the corners of Maureen's mouth. "You think Keegan is trying his hand at matchmaking again?"

"Yes, and don't sound so innocent," Clint scolded. "You suspected as much before I left last night, didn't you?"

She grinned. "It was pretty obvious. To everyone but you, evidently. So what happened?"

He paused, frowning. "We had dinner together. We talked. I told her about my life in New York. About Kristin—"

"You talked to her about Kristin?" Maureen sounded surprised. "I've never heard you talk about Kristin to anyone."

"I don't know why I did. It just seemed..."

"Natural?"

"Yeah." He looked up, and Maureen nodded knowingly. "Anyway, she told me that she'd come to Cooper's Corner two years ago to recuperate from a serious automobile accident. Evidently, she was in a coma after the crash, and when she came out of it, she had amnesia."

Maureen's brows lifted. "Amnesia? Wow." She grew pensive. "I remember a case Dan and I worked on once. A woman was brought into Bellevue covered in blood. She wasn't injured, but she couldn't remember what had happened to her. She couldn't remember anything, including her name. The doctor who treated her said she was suffering from hysterical amnesia. Something traumatic had caused her to block out all her memories, including her identity."

"What happened?"

Maureen shrugged. "Turned out she was faking it. The blood on her clothing belonged to her husband. We found his body stuffed in a car trunk at the airport. She'd devised the amnesia story to try and get away with murder."

Clint's gaze met hers. "You're not suggesting Beth is faking her amnesia, are you? For two years?"

"I'm not suggesting anything. I'm just saying that amnesia is a tricky thing."

"How do you mean?"

"Think about it," she insisted. "If her memory loss is genuine, Beth has a whole past she knows nothing about. Which means you don't know anything about it, either."

"That's...not entirely true," he said slowly. "That's what I wanted to talk to you about." He related everything Beth had told him, and when he finished, Maureen was looking more uneasy by the moment.

"I don't like the sound of this, Clint."

"There could be a legitimate explanation for everything. The gun, the money. Why the briefcase was the only thing recovered on that mountain. Maybe Beth *was* in danger. Maybe she was running from someone who wanted to kill her. That doesn't necessarily mean she did something bad. She could be an innocent victim in all this."

"You seem to be working awfully hard to convince me of that," Maureen pointed out. "Or are you trying to convince yourself?"

He sighed. "I don't know."

"Clint, what exactly is it you want me to do?"

"I don't know that, either. I thought you could make some calls. Maybe talk to the police in San Bernardino County. Find out everything they know."

"You mean, find out if Beth is telling you the truth?" she asked gently.

Clint tightened his lips. "That's not what I mean. I believe her, Maureen."

"And that's exactly what worries me." She leaned across the table, putting her hand over his. "Listen to yourself, Clint. You're desperately trying to convince both of us that Beth is the nice, sweet woman she appears to be. But the truth is, you don't know. If she really has amnesia, even *she* doesn't know. Maybe you're right. Maybe she is an innocent victim. Maybe she saw something she shouldn't have. It happens. Maybe that's why she was on the run that night. But,

Clint, you're forgetting something pretty important here. Even if she's innocent, she still has a past."

"I know that."

"Do you? Have you thought about what that means?" Maureen sat back and studied him for a moment. "Supposing you and Beth were to get close. Supposing she was to become an important part of your life. And Keegan's life. What happens if she gets her memory back? What happens if she remembers she has another family somewhere? A husband. Children. There's a very good possibility that she would decide to go back to that family. And where would that leave you? Where would it leave Keegan? He's already lost one mother. Do you really want to take a chance on putting him through that again?"

She was right, damn her, and Clint had known what she'd say before he ever sat down to talk to her. Maybe the reason he'd wanted to talk to Maureen in the first place was to have his own doubts confirmed, even if another part of him stubbornly clung to the memory of last night. The way Beth had felt in his arms. The way she'd kissed him so passionately...

What was it she'd said earlier? *Forget last night. Pretend it was just a dream.*

A beautiful, impossible dream...

CHAPTER NINE

THE NEXT DAY, Bryan's mother dropped the boys off at the movie theater in Williamstown while she ran errands and had a late lunch with a friend. Bryan and Keegan had been excited all week at the prospect of finally seeing the new Jon Wakeman sci-fi thriller, but by the time they neared the front of the line, the show was completely sold out.

A couple of girls from Keegan's school were in line ahead of them, and on a whim, he and Bryan decided to get tickets for the show they were going to see. But five minutes into the movie, Keegan realized what a mistake that had been. *After the Rain* was definitely not his kind of movie. Finally, after a long, torturous hour, he couldn't stand it any longer. He leaned over to suggest to Bryan that they leave, but then a song started to play in the movie and he stopped. He stopped dead still.

That was Beth's song.

The one she played every night in the gathering room to finish her set, only now it had lyrics. It always made Keegan a little sad when he heard Beth play that particular song, although he had no idea why.

So...if they were playing her song in a movie, did

that mean she was secretly rich and famous? Did she know movie stars? Could she get autographs?

Just as Keegan was warming to the notion of knowing someone with Hollywood connections, Bryan said in a loud whisper, "This movie is really stupid." He turned to Keegan. "Let's get out of here before someone sees us watching it."

Keegan was about to agree when one of the girls in front of them spun around in her seat and loudly shushed them. Bryan flicked a kernel of popcorn at her, which lodged in her hair, and of course she had to retaliate. Before long, popcorn was flying fast and furiously, and an usher came rushing up the aisle to shine a flashlight beam in their faces. He was pelted with kernels the moment he turned his back, and the girls started to giggle like crazy.

Everything considered, the afternoon wasn't a total bust, Keegan decided.

CLINT WAS WORKING in one of the outbuildings when Keegan got home that afternoon. He came strolling down the path, humming what sounded suspiciously like one of the tunes Beth always played in the gathering room. Which was odd, Clint thought. Beth's music was definitely not Keegan's style.

But that particular song always lingered in Clint's mind, too, long after Beth had finished playing. The melody was soulful and haunting, and he'd never heard a song that affected him in quite the same way. He'd never heard it anywhere else, either. He'd always wondered if it was Beth's own composition, but for some reason, he'd never bothered to ask her. The song seemed so poignant and intimate, it would have seemed a little like prying to question her about it.

Clint spotted Keegan out the dusty window and paused in his work to watch him. Keegan was tall for his age, with the lean, muscular physique of an athlete. He walked with the grace of an athlete, too, and he had an air of confidence even at thirteen. He was a good-looking kid, Clint thought proudly, especially now that he had a decent haircut. Back in the city—

Clint frowned. No need to think about those days anymore. The rough spots were behind them. Keegan was a different kid, a responsible kid. He always did his chores, went out of his way to be polite to the guests, and he was never cross or rude to the twins. Well, almost never. The twins were a challenge for anyone, but most of the time Keegan handled them with finesse.

He's happy, Clint thought, studying Keegan's face as he approached the shed. Clint's heart swelled with love, and suddenly, he wanted nothing more than to put his arms around his boy and hold him close, keep him safe for as long as he was able to.

As he watched Keegan, Maureen's warning last night came back to him.

What happens if Beth gets her memory back? What happens if she remembers she has another family somewhere? A husband. Children. There's a very good possibility that she would decide to go back to that family. And where would that leave you? Where would it leave Keegan? He's already lost one mother. Do you really want to take a chance on putting him through that again?

That warning had kept Clint tossing and turning all

night, and it had kept him from going to see Beth again today. He didn't want to turn his back on her, especially if she was in any danger. He'd do anything in the world to protect her, but his first priority had to be Keegan. He had to look out for his son's well-being. Clint had shirked that responsibility once before, and the result had almost been disastrous. He would never put Keegan second to his own needs again. Or to anyone else's.

Whatever he might have had with Beth was never going to be. Clint had best just accept that and get on with his life.

Keegan opened the door to the shed and glanced in. "Dad? You in here?"

"Hi, Son. How was the movie?"

"It totally sucked, Dad. *Dark Planet* was sold out so we had to see something else. That movie with Julia Ryan or somebody." He made a face. "Can you believe they actually make whole movies about people falling in love? How stupid is that?"

"Son, whole books have been written about people falling in love." Clint wiped his brow. "Sounds to me like you boys saw a chick flick."

"It was really lame. But you know what? They played Beth's song in it. Pretty cool, huh?"

Clint dropped his arm from his face. "What?"

"Yeah, you know that song she plays when she's almost finished? The sad one? They played that in the movie, only this time it had words and everything."

"It was the same music? You're sure?"

"Yeah, I'm positive. I even thought for a while that Beth might be secretly rich and famous, and she's just, you know, hiding out here for some reason. Wouldn't that be cool?''

Clint's heart was pounding a little too hard for comfort. As casually as he could, he asked, ''Did you see the credits for the music?''

''Nuh-uh. We didn't stay for the whole movie. But it would be pretty awesome, wouldn't it, if Beth knew a bunch of stars and stuff like that?''

Keegan rambled on for a few more minutes, but Clint wasn't really listening. His own mind was racing. Was it possible that Beth *didn't* have amnesia? Was it possible she really was hiding out in Cooper's Corner for some reason?

I've been running for two years. I realize that now. I thought I had a home here, a new life, but I was only fooling myself. All I've been doing is biding my time…until my past catches up with me. And now it has.

Who are you, Beth? Clint silently wondered. *And who or what are you running from?*

CLINT STAYED for the entire movie, but he couldn't remember a thing about the plot. It was the typical boy-meets-girl-boy-loses-girl affair, the kind of story that had made the lead actress famous. The song—Beth's song—came near the end, when all seemed lost for the luminous heroine. Heartbroken, she strolled alone in a snowy Central Park while the haunting song played in the background. Clint listened closely to the lyrics, trying to imagine Beth singing them, but it wasn't her voice resonating from the powerful speakers. He instantly recognized the artist. The woman was famous. And she was singing Beth's song.

As the music reached a crescendo, the hair on the back of Clint's neck stood on end. Beth had written those words, that music. He knew it with every fiber of his being. That song was a part of her. He could see her lovely face as she played it. He could see the loneliness in her eyes, the hurt and disillusionment as she felt that music deep within. Those same emotions were mirrored on the actress's face.

Looking at her was like a glimpse into Beth's soul. Clint almost felt as if he were intruding on Beth's privacy, and he had no right to. But he couldn't tear himself away. He had to hear it all. He had to find out her name.

He sat very still as he watched the closing credits. The name of the song was the same as the movie, "After the Rain." Music and lyrics by Valerie Lake.

All the way home, he couldn't get that name out of his head. Valerie Lake. Valerie Lake.

It was like a mantra, a chant that kept conjuring Beth's image. The dark, glossy hair with the unusual white streak at her widow's peak. The violet blue eyes fringed with dark lashes.

Valerie Lake.

The exotic name seemed to fit her.

Was she Valerie Lake? But how could a woman write a song that was performed by one of the hottest artists in the music business, a song destined to become a smash hit, and then just disappear? How was it that her family, her agent, *someone* hadn't combed the countryside looking for her?

Maybe they had. Maybe Beth had done such a thorough job of vanishing that no one had been able to find her. Until now.

Clint scowled at the road. Could she be faking the amnesia, as Maureen suggested? It was possible, of course, but he didn't think that was the case. He'd seen the agony and confusion in her eyes. And the fear. It was obvious Beth was a woman in turmoil, but then...he'd been fooled before, hadn't he? And by a woman he'd known and loved for years. Beth was a virtual stranger to him. He had no reason to trust her except...he did.

Somehow he did.

CLINT WENT STRAIGHT to his office when he returned to Twin Oaks, and logged on to the Internet. He plugged the name Valerie Lake into a search engine, then stared at the screen in amazement at the number of hits he'd gotten. One by one, he clicked on the links, scanning and then printing the information as a bizarre and troubling story began to unfold.

Valerie Lake was a songwriter and music composer who'd garnered critical acclaim and financial success over the years. She'd led a quiet life in her home in Los Angeles until two years ago when she became the victim of a stalker, a deranged woman named Rose Campbell who claimed Valerie had stolen songs from her. Rose seemed to know the antistalking laws well enough to elude the police, but one night, she crossed the line. She gained access to Valerie's home, held the terrified woman at gunpoint and forced her to open her safe. Rose stole ten thousand dollars in cash, claiming it was her due, then tried to kill Valerie.

Valerie's personal assistant, a young woman named Annie Lockhart, was working late that night and heard the gunshots. She rushed upstairs, but Rose had vanished. She was never found, but Valerie was so terrified by the incident that she fired her entire staff—including this Annie Lockhart—sold her house and left L.A. for good.

She went into seclusion, and no one knew what had happened to her until she surfaced a year later in Mystique, a quaint little town in the Texas Hill Country near Austin. Even now, with "After the Rain" destined to become a huge hit, she remained a recluse, refusing to grant so much as a telephone interview. She was afraid, some speculated, that if she were once again in the limelight, Rose Campbell would come after her.

Clint logged off and stared at the now blank computer screen. He felt stunned, blindsided by what he'd read. Rose Campbell had stolen ten thousand dollars from Valerie Lake's safe, then disappeared with the money.

They were convinced that it was all tied together somehow—the money in the briefcase, the gun, the missing bullets, my being alone on a mountain road in the middle of a rainstorm. They think I was running from someone, or from something I'd done.

Clint sat back in his chair, eyes closed, sighing deeply. He couldn't remember ever having felt so torn in his life. A part of him wanted to rush to Beth, confront her with everything he'd learned, and force the truth from her.

Another part of him, a stronger part, wanted to take

her in his arms and protect her—from her past and from the truth.

But what was the truth? Could "After the Rain" really be the key to her past? Or was it just a coincidence that she knew the song? Was it just a coincidence that both Valerie Lake and Rose Campbell had disappeared two years ago, at the same time Beth had moved to Cooper's Corner?

According to the articles he'd read online, Valerie Lake had turned up in Texas a year later. She was living as a recluse outside Austin.

So where was Rose Campbell, the stalker and would-be murderer?

Was she living here in Cooper's Corner? Was she the woman Clint knew as Beth Young?

He couldn't believe it. He didn't want to believe it. And yet...

It tied together everything she'd told him and everything he'd learned—a little too neatly to discount.

BETH WASN'T EXPECTING to see Clint again, at least not so soon. She would have thought he'd need a few days to digest everything she'd told him, but when she answered her door that night, there he stood, looking as handsome as ever.

"Clint," she said with a little catch in her throat. "What are you doing here?"

His green gaze measured her solemnly. "We need to talk."

"Didn't we say all there was to say last night?"

"Apparently not." He paused, his gaze still on her. "May I come in?"

His tone was formal and stilted, and Beth grew

more nervous by the moment. Silently, she stepped back, and with a slight nod, Clint brushed past her. Shoving his hands into his jeans pockets, he waited for her to close the door, and then as she turned, he said, "I've learned something."

Her heart bounced painfully against her chest. "About me?"

"Maybe." He nodded toward the sofa. "Let's sit down."

Now it was Beth who didn't like the sound of that ominous suggestion. She complied without question, though, taking one end of the sofa while he took the other. Far from looking relaxed, Clint sat perched on the edge of the seat, as if he might leap to his feet and begin to pace at any moment.

Or as if he might flee, Beth thought with a sinking feeling in her stomach. "What is it, Clint? You're scaring me."

He turned then, his gaze deep and probing. "Does the name Valerie Lake mean anything to you?"

Her response was automatic. "No, I don't think so. Why?"

"What about Rose Campbell?"

Beth flinched. "Rose Campbell?"

His gaze turned even darker. "You know that name?"

"No…I don't think so."

"But you reacted to it." His tone was almost accusing.

Beth's mouth went suddenly dry with fear. "Who is she?"

"Let me start at the beginning. Keegan and Bryan went to the movies today in Williamstown. They saw a picture called *After the Rain.* You've probably seen trailers for it on TV, but what they didn't include in the previews was a song toward the end. It's also called 'After the Rain,' and it was written by a woman named Valerie Lake.''

Beth was starting to feel very cold. ''I don't understand. What does that have to do with me?''

His green eyes studied her closely. '''After the Rain' is the song you play every night to end your set. Do you remember where you might have heard it?''

''I have no idea.'' Almost of their own will, Beth's hands clenched into fists. ''It was the first song I played after I was released from the hospital. When I sat down at Addie's piano, it…just came to me.'' She paused, biting her lip. ''You're not suggesting…I could be this Valerie Lake, are you?''

''That's one possibility.'' Clint got up and walked over to the window to glance out. When he turned, there was something in his eyes that made Beth's blood go cold.

''What is the other possibility?'' She wasn't at all certain she wanted to know.

''Valerie Lake is a songwriter who lived in California until two years ago. She was terrorized by a stalker named Rose Campbell.''

When Beth gasped, he gazed at her for a long moment from across the room. ''You reacted to that name again.''

''Maybe I was reacting to what you said about her,'' Beth said defensively, but the name immediately conjured an image of the rose that had been left on her doorstep. She got up and walked over to Clint. "There's more, isn't there?"

He glanced back out the window. "Rose Campbell claimed that Valerie had stolen some songs from her. She broke into Valerie's house one night and held her at gunpoint. She forced Valerie to open her safe, and Rose took ten thousand dollars in cash. She shot at Valerie twice before fleeing with the money, and the police were never able to find her."

Beth could literally feel the blood draining from her face. "Go on."

"Valerie was so terrified that Rose was able to breach her security system, she sold her house, fired her agent, her personal assistant, anyone who might have given the woman access to her home. Then she just disappeared. She resurfaced a year later in a small town near Austin, Texas. According to the articles I read, she's a recluse. All her business is conducted through her attorney, a man named Walter Cummings, who lives in Austin."

Beth's mind was churning with everything Clint had told her. She drew a ragged breath. "If Valerie Lake is living in Texas, obviously I'm not her. So where does that leave me, Clint?"

"All this could be just a coincidence," he said almost furiously. "We don't have any proof that you're even connected to this, except for..."

"Except for the money," she finished for him. "And the gun. Rose Campbell stole ten thousand dollars at gunpoint. That same amount of money, along with a gun, was found in a briefcase belonging to me on the side of the mountain the night I crashed my car."

"We don't know that the briefcase belonged to you," Clint said. "It was found on the side of the mountain. You said the police had their doubts as to how it had gotten there."

"Regardless of how it got there, it had my fingerprints on it," she said numbly. "And everything you've just described happened two years ago, before I came to Cooper's Corner. I'd say that's one too many coincidences. And that's not even counting the song. If it's only now been released, where would I have heard it? Did I hear Valerie play it the night I broke into her house? Did I steal that from her, too?" Beth whirled, no longer able to face Clint. "It all makes sense. It all fits. You know it does."

He moved up behind her and put his hands on her arms. Beth wanted nothing more than to lean against him, to take comfort in his strength and his steadiness. But she couldn't. She couldn't do that to him. She couldn't let him get any more involved than he already was, because if she was this Rose Campbell, if she had committed a robbery and attempted murder...

She shuddered, and when Clint tried to pull her closer, it was all she could do to resist. She closed her eyes, drawing on her own willpower, praying that for once in her life she would have the strength to do the right thing.

"I want you to go now."

"Beth—"

"I mean it, Clint." She turned then and gazed up at him. "I want to be alone. I need to think about everything you've told me. I have to figure out what to do."

He frowned down at her. "What do you mean?"

"If I'm Rose Campbell, then the police are still looking for me." When his frown deepened, she said harshly, "Surely you'd thought of that."

A flicker in his eyes told her that he had. And that he had his own dilemma to consider. "I still say we're jumping to a lot of conclusions here."

"Maybe. But I think some of those conclusions are obvious, and I think you believe that, too, Clint, or you never would have come here tonight."

WHEN CLINT GOT HOME, he found Maureen in the office, going through some paperwork. She looked up when he came in, smiled briefly, then went back to her sorting.

"Have you seen Keegan?" Clint asked absently.

"He's reading the twins a bedtime story."

"Let me guess. Max Danger?"

Maureen grinned. "We compromised on *The Adventures of Young Indiana Jones.*"

"Next thing you know, they'll be digging up your rose garden, looking for artifacts," Clint muttered.

"No doubt." Maureen went back to her work, and Clint started to pace. He caught her glancing up at him every so often, but she didn't comment on his restlessness. She seemed content to wait him out, which was unusual for Maureen. Patience was never her virtue.

Finally, Clint strode across the room and sat down in a chair opposite the desk. "I want to talk to you about something."

She glanced up briefly. "I'm listening."

"Remember the other day when you suggested this

might be a good month for us to each take some time off?''

''I remember.''

''I'd like to take you up on that,'' Clint said. ''I need a couple of days off.''

''Oh?'' She looked up, all innocence. ''When did you want to leave?''

''Tomorrow.''

''Tomorrow?'' She looked surprised, but somehow Clint didn't think she was.

''Is that a problem?''

''I don't think so. The kids and I can hold down the fort until you get back. If need be, I can always call Bonnie or Wendy to help out.''

Her easy acceptance made Clint suspicious. He lifted a brow. ''Just like that? No questions asked?''

Maureen shrugged. ''I assume it's important, or you wouldn't be springing this on me on such short notice.'' She paused, then glanced up. ''I also assume it has something to do with these.'' She held up the sheaf of papers he'd printed earlier from the Internet. ''And these have something to do with Beth, don't they?''

Clint sighed. ''Did you read them?''

''I scanned them before I realized what they were. I wasn't trying to pry. You left them scattered all over the desk.''

''It's all right. I'm not trying to keep anything from you,'' he said wearily.

''Then why don't you tell me what's going on? What's all this about, Clint?'' Maureen held the papers out to him. ''What does this Valerie Lake person have to do with Beth?''

He shrugged. "Maybe nothing. That's what I want to find out." He told her then about the song in the movie, and how he'd come home, after hearing it for himself, to do some research on the Internet. Maureen seemed to grow increasingly uneasy as the story progressed.

"So you're going all the way to Texas to talk to this woman, this Valerie Lake?"

"What else can I do? If I don't go down there and talk to her, Beth will. And I have a feeling she could be walking into trouble."

"So could you," Maureen pointed out.

"I can take care of myself."

"And what if you find out that Beth is this other woman...this Rose Campbell? What if you find out she's the one who stole that money, the one who tried to kill Valerie Lake? Can you handle that? What would you do, Clint? Call the police?"

He got up, suddenly angry, and started to pace again. "I don't know what I would do, okay? All I know is that Beth and I both need some answers, and Valerie Lake seems to be our only lead."

Maureen leaned across the desk, eyeing him intently. "Are you sure you know what you're doing? Are you sure you want to get even more involved in Beth's life than you already are? It could get ugly."

He turned in frustration. "What am I supposed to do, Maureen? You tell me. If Beth's in trouble, how can I turn my back on her? What kind of man would I be if I did that?"

"A smart one," Maureen said grimly. "But you wouldn't be the brother I know."

CHAPTER TEN

CLINT'S MIND WAS MADE UP. He was going to Texas.

First thing the next morning he made all the arrangements, and then he went to talk to Keegan about his plans. He didn't give his son any specifics, just that he was going to be out of town for a day or two, and was relieved when Keegan accepted the vague explanation without a lot of questions.

Next, Clint went by the library to talk to Beth. He'd debated on whether or not he should tell her what he was up to, but in the end, his conscience won out. He couldn't go poking around in her past, in her *life*, without her consent.

But when he got to the library that morning, Lisa Darnell informed him that Beth had gone away for a few days.

"A family emergency, she said."

"Did she say where she was going?" Clint pressed.

Lisa shook her head. "She didn't say. But I heard her on the phone making reservations. She said something about Austin. That's in Texas, right?"

Clint thanked her and started to hurry out of the library when Lisa called after him. "Mr. Cooper?"

He turned.

"I don't know if this helps or not, but she asked

for a one-way ticket. I thought that was kind of strange.''

Strange and disturbing, because evidently, Beth didn't plan on coming back.

BETH WAS EXHAUSTED. Her flight out of Logan had been delayed because of bad weather, which meant that she'd missed her connection in Dallas. Then, once she'd finally arrived in Austin, she'd had trouble renting a car. She'd gotten lost twice on her way out of the city, missed her exit off I-35 and was almost halfway to San Antonio before she realized her mistake. By the time she pulled up in front of the Flamingo Motel in Mystique, it was late afternoon.

The place looked like something from an old Route 66 poster. A six-foot flamingo in shocking-pink neon hovered on the roof over the office doorway, while a flock of the plastic variety adorned the grounds.

The flamboyant motel, like the rest of Mystique, seemed completely out of character for a small Texas town. As Beth had driven slowly through the narrow streets, she'd been amazed at how different the reality of the place was from her anticipation of it. On the long flight from Boston, she'd imagined varying shades of brown, dust and tumbleweeds, nothing much on the horizon but a scraggly mesquite tree or cactus.

But Mystique was a beautiful little town, nestled in the rolling landscape of the Texas Hill Country. The quaint stucco houses that lined the shaded streets were painted in pastels and trimmed with window boxes spilling over with impatiens. The main thoroughfare was cobblestone, protected by a thick canopy of leaves that blocked all but faint patches of sunlight.

Beth could see why the town would be attractive to an artist seeking peace and quiet to create. Or one needing to escape a terrifying episode with a mad-woman, she thought grimly as she got out of her car and strode up the walkway to the motel office.

The man behind the desk was tall and lanky, with an easy smile and a curious stare. His blue Western shirt and buff-colored Stetson were the first real touches of Texas that she'd seen. He lazily tipped back the brim of his hat as he waited for the machine to accept Beth's credit card.

"There you go," he drawled, pushing a registration form and her credit card across the desk toward her. "Just sign here and you'll be all set. I've put you in Room 11. It's got a real nice view of the pool."

"Thanks." Beth picked up her credit card and returned it to her purse.

"My name's Eddie, by the way. Eddie Barksdale. I own the place, so I'm here most of the time. You have trouble finding the ice machine or anything, you give me a shout."

"Thanks, I will." Beth headed for the door, then turned suddenly as something occurred to her. "Mr. Barksdale—"

"Call me Eddie. Mr. Barksdale is my daddy."

Beth smiled. "Eddie, then. I'm looking for some-one…an acquaintance. Her name is Valerie Lake. Do you know her?"

"Valerie Lake." He thought for a moment. "Name rings a faint bell, but I can't place her."

"She's a musician, a songwriter. She moved here about a year ago."

He shook his head. "We get a lot of artistic types around here, but they pretty much keep to themselves. Don't mingle much with the rest of us."

"Well, thanks anyway."

He touched the brim of his hat in response, and Beth gave a final wave before exiting the office and walking back out to her car. She got in and sat for a moment. Was it possible she was in the wrong town? But how many communities named Mystique could there be in Texas, particularly in such close proximity to Austin? This had to be the right place. Maybe Valerie Lake kept such a low profile that the locals still didn't know her.

But someone *had* to know her. Someone around here would know where she lived. Beth just had to talk to the right person.

She backed out of her parking space, and as she circled around the front drive, she glanced in the window. She could see Eddie behind the counter. He had the phone to his ear, and for a split second, Beth had the oddest notion that he was talking to someone about her.

Beth had originally planned to wait until the following morning to try to contact Valerie Lake, but when she stopped in at a diner near the motel for a cup of tea, she found the waitress—a thirty-something redhead—more than willing to pass the time of day with her. The place was almost empty, Beth noticed. The woman was probably bored.

"Valerie Lake? I know of her, but I don't know

her personally,'' Darla responded when Beth queried
her. ''She bought Earl Hanhardt's house from his kin
after he died. Must have been a year or so ago now.''
She paused. ''It's kind of a coincidence you should
ask me about her. My aunt Birdie works for her. She
goes out there a couple of times a week, does some
light housekeeping and a little cooking. The rest of
the time I guess the woman does for herself. She sure
doesn't come in here to eat.''

Beth stirred sweetener in her tea. ''Do you think
you could give me directions to her house?''

''Oh, sure,'' Darla said breezily. ''Her place is real
easy to find. You just follow Main Street all the way
out of town to where it turns into a gravel road. They
call it Old Hanhardt Road, because Earl lived out
there for so long. I have to warn you, though, if
you're going out there alone, the road is real isolated,
kind of spooky even. You'll think you're in the middle of nowhere. No neighbors or anything, just an old
sawmill, but it's closed down now. You'll see it on
the left, just before you get to the house. No one much
goes out there anymore except kids looking for a
thrill. The place is supposed to be haunted, on account
of someone was killed there.''

The waitress had gotten way off track, but Beth
knew better than to rush her. ''What happened?'' she
murmured politely.

Darla rested a hip against the corner of the booth,
settling in for a nice long chat. ''This was years ago,
but a bunch of teenagers went out there one night to
climb the sawdust piles. You'll see them—the piles,
that is—when you go out that way. Some of them
must be twenty-five feet high or more. Anyway, back

when the mill was operating, the sawdust used to catch fire underneath because of all the heat, so the piles were real dangerous. But kids being kids, they got to daring each other to climb them. One of them got all the way to the top, but when he started down, the sawdust collapsed and he fell through. It was so hot underneath, he burned to death before anyone could get to him. People say you can still hear him scream sometimes when you drive by the mill."

Beth shuddered. "How awful."

"Oh, it was bad all right. They had his funeral at the high school. Whole town turned out."

Beth found the gruesome story disturbing, so she said gently, "Well, thank you for the directions."

"Hey, no problem." Darla eyed her curiously. "She a friend of yours, if you don't mind my asking?"

"Not exactly," Beth hedged. "We have…a mutual acquaintance. I thought I might stop by and just say hello."

"Well, I hope you haven't made the trip for nothing. From what I hear, she doesn't exactly cotton to visitors. Aunt Birdie says she's practically a hermit."

"She doesn't have family or friends here in town?"

Darla shrugged. "Not that I know of. But it's not so unusual that she'd move here all by herself. A lot of artists are attracted to the Hill Country. Painters, sculptors, we've even got an actor or two living around here. The best I remember, Valerie stayed over at the Flamingo for a few days until her lawyer was able to close on the Hanhardt house. A couple of weeks later, she moved in."

Beth frowned. "She stayed at the Flamingo Motel?"

"I'm pretty sure."

"Then why..."

"Why, what?"

Beth shook her head. "Nothing." She didn't want to mention it to Darla, but she had to wonder why Eddie had told her he didn't know Valerie. Had he deliberately misinformed her, or did he just not remember the woman? Beth supposed it was possible that Valerie had registered under an assumed name if she'd been trying to remain incognito.

Still, in a town as small as Mystique, it was hard to believe that Eddie Barksdale wouldn't have heard of Valerie even if she hadn't stayed at the Flamingo.

So why had he lied? And who had he been talking to just seconds after Beth left the motel office?

RATHER THAN GOING BACK to the Flamingo to confront Eddie, Beth decided to take a drive out to Valerie's house just to see if she could find the place. She had no idea what she would do once she got there. Walk up to the front door and ring the bell? Look her straight in the eye and say, "Hello. Remember me? I think I may be Rose Campbell, the woman who stole ten thousand dollars from you and then tried to kill you."

And if Valerie confirmed her worst suspicions, what would she do then? Wait for the police to come and take her away in handcuffs?

Just take it one step at a time, Beth cautioned herself. She had to keep a level head about her, and it wouldn't help if she kept imagining the worst case scenario. After all, wasn't it possible the woman wouldn't even recognize her? Wasn't it possible that Beth had no connection whatsoever to Valerie Lake or Rose Campbell?

It was possible...but deep down, Beth didn't think it very likely.

Following Darla's directions, she took Main Street to the outskirts of town, where it turned into a gravel road. She was suddenly in the country, and the waitress had been right: the road was very isolated, crowded on either side by thick tangles of vines and scrub.

The light was fading rapidly, and Beth knew that darkness would soon fall. Night creatures would start to prowl. She glanced around and shivered. What kind of wild animals roamed the nearby woods? Coyotes, wolves, bobcats? She had no idea, but she decided it probably hadn't been such a great idea to come out here so close to nightfall.

The sawmill was just ahead and to her left. She could see the huge mounds of sawdust eerily silhouetted in the deepening twilight. Darla was right, she thought. They did look like small mountains.

As Beth drove by the mill, an eerie feeling settled over her. She wondered if the sawdust, even after all this time, still smoldered beneath the surface, if the call of some distant night bird was really a scream....

She was being foolish, she scolded herself. It was just a sad, tragic story, one that had been undoubtedly embellished in the retelling over the years. There was nothing to fear from the sawmill or its resident ghost. Beth's real worry was located about a half mile up the road.

The house was to her left, on the same side of the road as the sawmill. An address was stamped on the mailbox, but the name was missing. A fence surrounded the property, and an electronic gate guarded the lane that wound a quarter of a mile or so back to the modest ranch-style house, which stood shrouded by trees.

Beth pulled to the side of the road, parked and got out. The evening was warm and balmy, but there seemed to be a slight chill in the breeze that rustled through the trees. As she stood staring at the house, that same odd feeling came over her, and she was suddenly certain that someone was watching her.

But no one was around. She was letting her imagination get the better of her. The trees encircling the house would impede the view of the road. No one could see her.

Still, if someone was standing at one of the windows, staring in the right direction...

Or if someone was standing atop one of the sawdust mounds...

Imagination or not, Beth found herself hurrying back to the car, climbing in and locking the doors. She sat for a moment, waiting for the eerie sensation to fade, but when she couldn't shake it, she started the car and drove slowly past the front gate.

A few hundred yards up the road, she finally found a place to turn around, and headed back toward town. When she neared Valerie's drive, she saw that a long, dark-colored car with tinted windows had driven through the gate and was waiting to pull onto the road.

Beth slowed to give the car the right of way. It

didn't move. The vehicle remained in the drive until Beth had driven past, then pulled onto the road behind her.

She glanced in her rearview mirror. Twilight had fallen, but the vehicle behind her was driving without lights. The driver swerved into the other lane as if to pass her, and a terrible feeling of déjà vu gripped Beth.

She clutched the steering wheel as a blinding pain erupted behind her eyes. The road blurred in front of her, and in her mind, she saw another road, this one mountainous and slippery. Treacherous in the downpour as a vehicle behind her tried to pass. It was beside her suddenly, bumping her car, making her swerve violently to avoid a collision. Then, in horror, she felt her tires skid on the wet pavement, and the car spun completely around, until she was sliding backward down the mountain, toward the guard rail and the embankment....

Beth's heart was pounding so hard she could scarcely breathe. The mountain highway disappeared, and she found herself on the gravel road once again. But still in the throes of panic, she hit the brakes without thinking and screeched to a stop.

Which was a stupid thing to do, considering there was a vehicle behind her.

Bracing herself for the impact, Beth glanced in the rearview mirror. Then she turned to scan the darkening road behind her. Nothing was there.

The car had vanished.

BETH'S HANDS SHOOK so badly, she wasn't certain how she managed to drive back to town without mishap. She still didn't know what had happened to her. One moment a car had been behind her, and in the next instant, it was gone. One moment she had been driving on a gravel road, and in the next, she was careening out of control down a mountain pass.

Had the vision been real?

For just a brief moment in time, had the murky recesses of her mind cleared enough to give her a glimpse of what had happened to her the night of the accident? Had someone really tried to kill her?

But who?

And why?

Still trembling, she pulled into the parking lot at the motel and found a space near her room. There were only three or four other vehicles in the lot, including a black pickup truck near the office. Beth had noticed it earlier because of the striking paint job. Yellow-and-red flames licked over the hood and fender, as if the engine underneath was on fire. She wondered if it belonged to Eddie. Somehow he hadn't struck her as the flashy type.

But as she got out and studied the truck, she happened to glance toward the office. She hadn't realized before that the windows there looked out on her side of the motel. She could see someone behind the desk—Eddie, she supposed—and Beth had the distinct feeling that he was staring at her, watching her.

An uneasy chill slid up her spine. Had he put her on this side of the motel so that he could watch her coming and going?

Disconcerted by the notion, Beth turned and strode away from the motel. She didn't quite trust herself behind the wheel of her car so soon, but neither did she want to be alone in her room. She headed toward the diner half a block away.

A handful of customers were scattered about the restaurant, and when Beth walked in, most of them glanced up, studied her curiously for a moment, then went back to their coffee and meals.

She slipped into the nearest booth, and after a bit, Darla ambled over with a glass of water and a menu. "Back so soon?"

Beth nodded and smiled. "I didn't expect to find you still here. What time do you get off?"

Darla shrugged. "Oh, not for a couple more hours yet. One of the other waitresses didn't show up for her shift. I'm pulling a double, but it's not so bad. I can use the money." She slid a pencil from behind her ear and took her pad from the pocket of her apron. "You know what you want or do you need a minute to look at the menu?"

"Just a bowl of soup," Beth said. "Whatever you have is fine. And a cup of hot tea."

"Coming right up."

Darla disappeared into the kitchen, and Beth sat staring out the window. After a few moments, the bell over the door sounded and a man in a khaki uniform entered. He had a badge clipped to his left breast pocket and a gun belt slung low on his hips to accommodate the beginnings of a paunch. Standing just inside the doorway, he carefully removed his aviator-style sunglasses and slipped them into his shirt pocket.

His every move seemed slow, calculated, as if he were very aware of—and relished—the attention an officer of the law commanded. He nodded briefly to

Darla, who was coming out of the kitchen, then sauntered over to the counter and straddled a stool.

"That's Sheriff Gardner," Darla informed Beth as
she placed the bowl of soup in front of her. "He
comes in every day about this time for the blue plate
special and a cup of coffee."

No cause for alarm, Beth tried to tell herself as
Darla hurried away. The sheriff came in every day.
He hadn't been summoned. He wasn't suspicious.

But even as she tried to calm herself, her gaze went
back to the counter. The sheriff had his back to her,
but with a start, Beth realized he was watching her in
a mirror that hung on the wall behind the counter.

She almost dropped her soupspoon. She was suddenly so nervous she couldn't have lifted the utensil
to her mouth if her life depended on it.

Throwing some bills on the table, Beth tried to
walk calmly out of the diner, but it was difficult the
way her knees trembled. And her heart pounded so
hard she felt sure everyone must hear it.

Out on the street, she hurried toward the motel,
where the neon flamingo flickered splendidly in the
dusk. Beth wanted to appreciate the quirkiness of the
motel, the quaintness of the town, but all she could
think about were the dark alleys and side streets that
ran parallel to some of the businesses. She couldn't
walk by one without wondering if someone might be
lurking in the shadows, waiting for her. Or if the sheriff had sent some of his deputies to keep her under
surveillance.

Were those footsteps she heard behind her?

You're being paranoid, Beth scolded herself, but

she increased her pace, resisting the urge to turn and glance over her shoulder.

As she approached the motel, she finally did turn, and she could have sworn she saw a shadow dart behind one of the buildings. Or was that her imagination, too? Beth had no idea, but by this time, she'd worked herself into quite a state. She turned to flee to the safety of her room, but someone blocked her way.

CHAPTER ELEVEN

STRONG HANDS GRASPED her arms, and for a moment, Beth struggled to free herself.

"Hey, it's okay. It's me."

She stepped back, blinking in the near darkness. "Clint?" She couldn't believe her eyes. "What are you doing here?" And then, instead of waiting for an answer, she walked straight into his arms. He held her for a moment, his hand smoothing her hair.

When she just clung tighter, he said, "Not that I don't appreciate the welcome, but what's going on? Are you okay?" His voice vibrated in her ear, making her realize how very glad she was to see him.

"I thought someone was following me."

"Just now?" When she nodded, he pulled away. "Let me check it out."

Beth caught his arm. "No, don't. It was…it was probably just my imagination. I've been letting things get to me ever since I got here."

Clint frowned down at her briefly before his gaze scanned the street. "What do you mean?"

She related to him her excursion to Valerie's house, the weird feelings she'd experienced, the certainty that someone had been watching her. Then she told him about the car that had followed her from the drive, and the memory—if that's what it had been—of the car crash.

His expression hardened. "Then someone really did try to kill you that night."

"I can't be certain. I'm not even sure what I experienced earlier was a real memory. Maybe I imagined the whole thing, just like now, when I thought someone was following me. This isn't the first time I've seen things, Clint. A few nights ago at Twin Oaks, I could have sworn I saw someone staring through the window at me as I played."

"Was that the night I walked you to your car?"

"How did you know?" she asked in surprise.

"Because I think that's the night Keegan hatched his matchmaking plot. The twins told me he was outside spying on you, but *he* said that he and Bryan Penrose were just playing some kind of game for the girls' benefit. I'd be willing to bet he's the one you saw staring in the window at you."

But Beth wasn't convinced. "I don't know. That doesn't sound like Keegan."

"You haven't known him for as long as I have," Clint said dryly. "He's the same kid who gave you that phony note from Grace. Remember?"

"That night seems a million years ago," she said wistfully, wishing desperately that Keegan's covert schemes were the only intrigue in her life. "Clint—" She broke off when she noticed the window in the motel office. Was Eddie watching them even now?

Seeing her face, Clint glanced over his shoulder. "What's wrong?"

"Nothing. I was just wondering about something the owner of the motel told me earlier."

"You mean Eddie?" When Beth lifted her brows in surprise, Clint shrugged. "I met him when I registered. Seemed like a nice enough guy."

"I thought so, too, at first, but...wait a minute," Beth said in confusion. "You're staying at this motel? How did you know I was here?"

"The town only has three motels. I called around until I found you." The way he stared down at her made her heart beat even harder. His gaze seem to imply that it wouldn't have mattered if there'd been three hundred motels. He would have searched until he found her.

"So tell me about this Eddie character," he said. "What did he say to you?"

"The waitress at the diner told me that Valerie had stayed at the Flamingo when she first came to town. She even said Eddie had a thing for Valerie, but he told me he didn't know her."

"Why would he lie about it?" Clint glanced over his shoulder again.

Beth shrugged helplessly. "I have no idea."

"Why don't we just go in and talk to him? See what we can find out."

"I don't think that would be such a great idea. It might have been an honest mistake on his part, and besides, until I find out the whole story—about my connection to Valerie Lake and Rose Campbell, I mean—the less attention I call to myself, the better." She didn't come right out and say it, but the implication was that she didn't want to arouse suspicions, didn't want an outside party involving the police. Not yet.

Clint seemed to understand. He gave a brief nod of

agreement. "You have a point." He shot a wary glance toward the office. "Tell you what. Let's go back to one of the rooms and try to talk this whole thing out. See what we can come up with."

They crossed the parking lot to Beth's room, which was closer, and as she unlocked the door, Clint tried to lighten the mood. "Hey, at least you've got a nice view—if you don't mind plastic flamingos. My room faces the garbage bins around back. You think Eddie was trying to tell me something?"

Beth smiled, but a shiver slipped down her backbone. Clint's remarks had inadvertently reminded her of her earlier concern about the proximity of her room to the office, and the feeling that Eddie might be watching her. She didn't say a word to Clint, though. The whole idea sounded paranoid, even to her.

They walked inside, and Beth flipped on a light. Earlier, she'd barely noticed the accommodations, but she took a moment now to survey her surroundings. It was a typical motel room—plaster walls, framed scenes of Texas sunsets and bluebonnets, and a cotton print bedspread.

She hadn't unpacked yet, and Beth wondered now if that had been a subconscious decision on her part, an instinct to be prepared in the event a quick getaway was necessary.

That would be something Rose Campbell would do. A woman like her would think of such things.

Paranoid, Beth scolded herself. But she felt chilled just the same, and as she glanced at Clint and saw the concern in his eyes, she had to turn away before she rushed headlong into his arms again. "You shouldn't have followed me here,'' she said a bit harshly. ''I told you before I don't want you involved in this.''

His gaze darkened at her tone. ''I didn't follow you here. I'd already decided to come down here and see Valerie Lake on my own before I knew you were here.''

''But you shouldn't have,'' she insisted. ''You have to think about Keegan.''

Something flickered in his eyes, as if she'd hit a nerve, but it was gone in an instant, replaced by a stubborn resolve Beth was becoming all too familiar with. His easygoing demeanor belied a steely determination that could be formidable, she imagined, in business and in love. ''I am thinking about Keegan,'' he said with a deep frown. ''Believe me, I never stop thinking about Keegan. But that doesn't meant I can't care about you.''

His voice was so deep, so masculine. So seductive. That voice was going to be her undoing. Beth just knew it. ''I'll be fine. I can take care of myself.'' She turned, so that she could at least avoid his unwavering gaze.

''You can turn away from me, but it won't change anything. I'm not going anywhere, Beth. Like it or not, you need me here with you.''

''But I don't *want* you here.'' Her voice grew just as stubborn as his, but she feared it lacked the same conviction.

''That's what you say. But your eyes...'' He put his hand under her chin and turned her to face him. ''Your eyes tell me something very different.''

Don't, Beth wanted to beg him. *Don't look at me*

*that way. Don't let me know that you care. Don't...
kiss me.*

But it was too late. His head lowered and Beth
caught her breath as his mouth found hers. His kiss,
like his voice, was deep, dark, dangerously seductive.
He moved his lips against hers, coaxing her to respond, and when she did, their tongues tangled,
fought, mated. His arms were around her now, drawing her closer, pressing her against him until she
could feel how much he wanted her.

"Beth...Beth," he whispered against her mouth.
He tried to kiss her again, but her senses slowly came
back to her. She stepped away.

"Don't. Don't kiss me again." She put her hand
to her mouth. "I can't think when you kiss me like
that."

"Then don't think." He reached for her. "Let me
think for both of us."

From somewhere deep within she dredged up the
resolve to say firmly, "No. I can't do that. This is my
life, my responsibility. I have to do this myself." She
turned and walked over to the window to glance out.
"I still say you shouldn't have come."

"Yes, I got that message, loud and clear."

He was angry now, and Beth couldn't blame him.
She'd kissed him one moment, kissed him like she
could never have enough of him, and then she'd
pushed him away. How was he supposed to feel?

"Why does my wanting to help threaten you so
much?" he demanded.

"Because..." She clenched her hands into fists.
"Because what if I really am Rose Campbell? What
if I did all those terrible things the articles said she

did? I don't want to see your face when you find out the truth. When you learn the kind of person I was. And maybe the kind of person I still am." She turned, desperately seeking his gaze. "I wish I hadn't come here, either, Clint. I wish both of us could go back to Cooper's Corner and pretend we never heard of Valerie Lake or Rose Campbell. But we can't do that, can we?"

He ran a hand through his short hair, tangling it, and Beth thought that must be the way he looked in the mornings crawling out of bed. Hair all mussed. A shadow of a beard. So sexy she could hardly bear it. She could picture him smiling down at her, climbing back into bed at her invitation....

He didn't say anything, but their gazes clung for the longest moment, as if they were sharing an intimate secret, and then Clint broke the contact. He turned and started to pace restlessly about the room.

Beth wondered what he was thinking, if he was regretting his decision to come here, his offer to help her. She wondered if he was regretting the kiss and all it seemed to spark between them.

She glanced back out the window, but she could see his reflection in the glass.

"I did a lot of thinking on my way down here," he finally said. "There's something about this whole thing that doesn't seem right to me."

"What do you mean?"

"Think about it for a minute. Valerie Lake and Rose Campbell disappeared from Los Angeles at virtually the same time. Rose was never heard from again, and it was a year before anyone knew where Valerie had gone. Then she turns up here, in the middle of nowhere, practically a recluse. From what I've been able to gather, she doesn't have family here. No friends. Yet she shows up here one day and buys a house, as if she intends to stay for a very long time."

Beth frowned. "And?"

He paused, as if gathering his thoughts and trying to make sense of them. "Rose Campbell tried to kill Valerie before Rose disappeared. By all accounts, she was a troubled woman, a stalker who may have been delusional. That could be why she claimed Valerie had stolen some of her songs. To her, it wasn't just a claim. She really believed it. Maybe at some point she even became obsessed with Valerie. Who knows?"

Beth's scowl deepened. She still didn't know where he was going with this.

Clint gestured with his hand. "Okay, say she *was* obsessed with Valerie. Or maybe she even hated her. That would explain why Rose tried to kill Valerie. But if you are Rose," he said slowly, "then why did someone try to kill you?"

Beth's heart gave a funny little jump. He was starting to make a strange kind of sense. "Go on."

He stopped pacing and stared at her for a moment. "Let's assume that someone did try to kill you on the mountain that night. If you really are Rose Campbell, who would have wanted you dead?"

"Valerie?"

He shook his head. "I don't think so. If she was so terrified after Rose broke into her house that she had to go into hiding, would she really have the courage to go after her stalker?"

"Then who?" Beth asked helplessly.

Again his gaze held hers. "Supposing the woman who lives here is Rose Campbell."

"But...that's crazy," Beth blurted.

"Is it?" Clint resumed his pacing. "Rose stalked Valerie for a long time before she tried to kill her. She probably knew everything about her, every aspect of Valerie's life. Somehow she managed to lure Valerie to the mountain that night, plant evidence in her car linking her to Rose. Then she followed her down the mountain and tried to kill her a second time. Think about it, Beth. After the shooting incident at Valerie's house in L.A., Rose just disappeared. The authorities never found her. And now Valerie is a recluse."

"But what you're suggesting..." Was impossible to believe.

He smiled slightly. "What I'm suggesting is that you're Valerie Lake, not Rose Campbell."

Beth put a hand to her mouth, trying to curb her shock, trying to rein in the wild, unreasonable hope that surged through her. Was it possible? Could she really be Valerie Lake? Could she be Rose Campbell's victim, and not her alter ego?

"How else would you have known about 'After the Rain,'" Clint asked softly, "if you didn't write it?"

Beth wanted to believe him. More than anything else in the world, she wanted to believe him. Who wouldn't rather think of herself as a victim than a criminal? But the scenario was far-fetched, and they both knew it.

"Even if Rose planted her own identification in Valerie's car, how could she know that Valerie's fingerprints wouldn't be checked? Or her dental records? None of those things can be disguised,'' Beth argued.

Clint shrugged. "I thought of that. But from what you've told me, the place where your car went over the side of the mountain was pretty rugged and remote. Maybe Rose thought the body would never be found, or maybe she assumed a small sheriff's department wouldn't have the necessary resources and would just use the identification they found on the body or in the car, especially if Rose didn't have any next of kin. Without a criminal record, Valerie's fingerprints probably wouldn't have been on file anyway, and there's a good chance Rose's wouldn't be, either, because she was never arrested for the stalking or for the breaking and entering.''

"But what about the car?" Beth persisted. "Wouldn't it have been registered to Valerie? Rose couldn't have known beforehand that a mudslide would bury it.''

"No, that was just a lucky break. Or maybe it wasn't so lucky, because in all likelihood, she'd taken precautions with the car, too. Planted the money and the gun to convince the authorities Rose Campbell was the driver. Maybe she even somehow convinced Valerie to drive her car. Or maybe she changed the license plates, stole the registration…." He trailed off, shrugging again. "I'm not saying I know how she did it. I'm just saying it's possible that she did do it.''

"Okay, but apart from everything else we've talked about, there's another big hole in your theory," Beth said quietly. She lifted her gaze to Clint's. "Why didn't she come back and finish me off? She couldn't have known I'd have amnesia.''

"From the way you explained the crash, it was a miracle you survived. Maybe she just assumed you'd been killed."

"That seems a little careless for a woman who was clever enough to pull off an identity switch."

"There is yet another possibility." Clint's gaze seemed to darken. "She could have had someone watching you for the past two years, waiting to see if you got your memory back. Maybe she still had an obsession with Valerie, and on some strange level, she wanted Valerie to live as long as she wasn't a threat."

Beth shivered uncontrollably. The notion that someone, a stranger, might have been watching her every move, invading her privacy, and then reporting back to a madwoman...

Beth had felt so safe in Cooper's Corner. She wondered if she would ever feel safe anywhere now.

"Look, I know it sounds bizarre," Clint admitted. "But, my God, you only have to watch the news to hear of things far stranger than this. And when you think it through, it's not completely illogical. Valerie Lake isn't famous, and she's always been a bit of a loner. No close friends or family. But what she does have is a lot of money. And with the release of *After the Rain,* she's probably going to be set for life. If Rose was truly convinced that Valerie stole songs from her, maybe even stole *that* song, then she would feel entitled to Valerie's wealth."

Beth studied him for a moment. "Do you really believe any of this, Clint?"

"I think it's possible," he said stubbornly.

"Because you want to believe it," Beth insisted.

"Don't you see? The only thing we know for sure is that I'm not Beth Young. We have to face that, Clint. If it turns out that I'm not Rose Campbell or Valerie Lake, nothing really changes. I still won't be the woman you thought I was. I'll still have a past out there somewhere, and sooner or later, it'll catch up with me."

"Is that why you bought a one-way ticket to Austin?" he asked grimly. "You weren't planning to come back to Cooper's Corner no matter what you found out, were you?"

She gazed at him longingly, wishing she could touch his hand, his face. But she didn't dare. "Please try to understand. I was thinking about you and Keegan. I don't want to hurt you."

"You think it wouldn't hurt me if you just disappeared from my life?" He moved toward her. "I'm in love with you, Beth. Don't you know that?"

Her heart almost stopped. For a moment, she couldn't even breathe. All she could do was gaze at him in shock.

He…loved her?

Oh, God.

He loved her.

Her gaze raked his features. His eyes, his mouth… she loved the way he looked. She loved everything about him. She loved him….

Unable to help herself, she lifted her hand to his face, caressing his cheek with her fingertips. He caught her hand and brought it to his lips.

"If you don't want to hurt me, then don't run away from me, Beth."

"But—"

"No buts." He drew her toward him. "We're in this together, no matter what. Understood?"

She buried her face in his shoulder. She knew she should resist, but how could she? How could she send him away? How could she live without him?

Because you may have to, a little voice reminded her. *If you're Rose Campbell—*

No, she thought stubbornly. She wouldn't think about that now. Wasn't it just as possible that she was Valerie Lake, an innocent victim? A woman who had done nothing more than survive against all odds...

She squeezed her eyes closed as Clint's arms held her close. He was in love with her! She wanted to rejoice at the knowledge, revel in the fantasy that her dreams might yet come true.

But it was hard to find even a moment's joy when a dark premonition was quietly sweeping over her.

CLINT LAY ON HIS BACK, scowling at the ceiling. He hadn't wanted to leave Beth alone, even for a moment, but she'd insisted she needed some time to herself. To think.

"Don't worry," she'd assured him, her eyes shining with emotion. "I'm not running away. I'm not going anywhere...without you."

He'd dropped a kiss on her forehead. "Is that a promise?"

"Yes, it's definitely a promise."

But that had been the only encouragement she'd given him, he thought morosely. She hadn't told him she loved him, and she certainly hadn't invited him to stay the night. She'd been adamant about needing her space.

Maybe he shouldn't have revealed his own feelings quite so abruptly. He'd just blurted out his love for her in the heat of the moment, rather than holding something back. Rather than protecting his pride and his heart.

And if past experience was any indication, Clint knew he could be headed for serious heartbreak.

But…what the hell was he supposed to do? He was too old for games, too old to play coy, and besides, even if he pretended otherwise, he couldn't undo his feelings. He couldn't *unlove* Beth, no matter how hard he tried.

No matter who she turned out to be.

And that was the rub, wasn't it? He didn't really know the woman he'd fallen in love with. He didn't know anything about her except that she was beautiful and kind and—he would swear—incapable of violence.

She wasn't Rose Campbell. He was convinced of that.

But who was she? Valerie Lake? If she were indeed Valerie, what would that mean for them? For…him?

Valerie Lake was a talented, wealthy woman. If she chose, she could move in the jet-set circles of the entertainment industry. She could be—

He closed his eyes.

She could be like Kristin. Sophisticated, ambitious and…restless.

Don't borrow trouble, he warned himself, but he suddenly had a terrible feeling that history was about to repeat itself.

Propping himself against the headboard, he reached

for the phone and dialed the number for Twin Oaks, relaxing a bit when he heard his sister's voice.

"Maureen?"

"Clint! I'm so glad you called. I've been thinking about you all day." Her voice dropped slightly. "How are things down there? Did you find Beth?"

"We're staying at the same motel. Separate rooms," he added, because he knew she'd be wondering.

"Have you found out anything?"

"We've both asked around about Valerie Lake, but the locals don't seem to know much about her. She more or less showed up out of the blue and moved into a house a year ago without much fanfare. But there's something peculiar about all this, Maureen."

"We already know that much," she said dryly. "You didn't have to go all the way to Texas to figure that out."

Clint frowned. "I'm serious. I'm starting to get some strange vibes down here. I don't know how to explain it, but Beth feels it, too. She chalks it up to her imagination, but I'm not so sure. She drove out to Valerie's house earlier. Evidently it's in a pretty isolated area. The place is surrounded by a fence, and the drive has an electronic gate. She couldn't get near the house, but she said she had the distinct impression someone was watching her. She drove up the road to turn around, and when she came back, a car was waiting at the end of the drive. It followed her for a while, then just vanished."

"Cars don't just vanish, Clint."

"I realize that, but Beth had some sort of episode—"

"What kind of episode?" Maureen asked sharply.

"She may have remembered what happened the night of her accident."

"What do you mean, *may* have?"

Clint hesitated. "She's not sure it was a real memory. She's afraid she manufactured it."

"What do you think?"

"I think it was real," he said flatly. "Beth remembered another vehicle on the mountain with her that night. It forced her off the road. Her car crash wasn't an accident. Someone tried to kill her."

Maureen was silent for a moment. "Have you thought about going to the police down there?"

"We can't go to the police."

"How many times have I heard that?" Maureen said with a weary sigh. "And it's always for the wrong reason. In your case, I'd say you don't want to go to the police because you think there's a good chance that Beth is Rose Campbell. Am I right?"

"No," he said almost angrily. "I don't think she's Rose. But based on what we've got so far, that's exactly what the police would believe."

"I don't like this, Clint. God only knows what you've gotten yourself into down there. If someone tried to kill Beth and they find out she's still alive, what do you think is going to happen? They'll come after her again. And if you're in the way—"

"It'll be all right," he interrupted. "Have a little faith in your big brother."

"I do, but... I should be down there with you."

"You have a pretty full plate right where you are," he reminded her.

"I know." She sighed again. "How do we get ourselves into these messes, Clint?"

He gave a low laugh. "Beats me."

"I guess you can thank Keegan for your current predicament. If he hadn't wanted you and Beth together so badly, you might have kept right on pretending you had no feelings for her. You might have been home safe and sound at this very moment, still mooning over her."

Clint frowned. "Keegan just gave things a nudge, that's all. Beth and I would have gotten together sooner or later." Keegan had seen what Clint was too blind to see. Or too stubborn to admit. He and Beth were meant to be together.

"I guess you're probably right," Maureen reluctantly agreed. "But I'm still going to worry about you until you're home safe and sound."

"I know. That's why I called. I promised I'd stay in touch. Here, let me give you the number where I can be reached. I'm staying at the Flamingo Motel in Mystique." He gave her the phone number and his room number, and after she'd jotted them down, he said, "I have my cell phone with me, too, but I've been having trouble getting a signal down here. Tell Keegan I'll try to call him later, okay?"

"I will. But, Clint...?" She paused. "Promise me you'll be careful. I may no longer be on the force, but I still have a cop's instinct for danger. I have a bad feeling about all this. I'm afraid you're headed for trouble. Big trouble."

KEEGAN STEPPED BEHIND a door as his aunt got up from the desk and strode from the office. He watched her until she disappeared around a corner, and then, glancing both ways down the hall, he hurried into the office.

He knew from her end of the phone conversation that his dad had given her the number where he was staying. Keegan also figured, from what his aunt had said, that his dad was in some kind of trouble. Big trouble. And it was all Keegan's fault.

I guess you can thank Keegan for your current predicament.

If someone tried to kill Beth and they find out she's still alive, what do you think is going to happen? They'll come after her again. And if you're in the way…

I have a bad feeling about this.

Desperately, Keegan rifled through the papers on the desk, trying to hold back tears. *Stupid, stupid, stupid.* Why couldn't he have just left well enough alone? He and his dad had been happy enough, just the two of them. Why had he ever thought Beth Young was the perfect woman for his father?

He was stupid, that's why.

Finding the message pad, Keegan carefully copied down the information. He stared at the unfamiliar phone number for a moment. Flamingo Motel, Mystique, Texas.

Texas! Why was his dad in Texas? He didn't even know anyone there. So why had he gone? To save Beth? It sounded like she was in some kind of danger, too, and if his dad had gone there to rescue her, who was going to rescue him?

Keegan pounded his fist against his forehead. Why, why, *why* had he ever come up with such a stupid plan? Why had he spied on Beth that night? Why had he arranged for her and his dad to have dinner, and then put that rose on her doorstep in hopes that she'd think his dad had left it for her? The matchmaking Web site he'd visited for advice had said leaving a rose was romantic or something, but it was just stupid. Everything he'd done was stupid.

Including telling his dad about that stupid song he'd heard in that stupid, lame movie. Everything had started getting weird after his dad had heard about that song.

Keegan thought for a moment. Maybe that was it. Maybe his dad and Beth were in some kind of danger because of that song. But…why?

Think, dork!

Okay, his dad had been working out back when Keegan told him about the movie. He'd rushed off after that and Keegan hadn't seen him for hours. Then later that night, Keegan had come into the office to ask him something. His dad had been at the computer, concentrating so hard on whatever he was reading that he hadn't looked up when Keegan entered, hadn't responded to Keegan's question. Keegan hadn't thought much about it at the time because his dad sometimes spaced out like that when he was working at his drafting table. But now Keegan wondered what his dad had been doing on the computer. If it had anything to do with Beth and that song. If it had anything to do with his dad being in Texas.

Keegan logged on to the Internet with grim resolve. He'd gotten his dad into this mess. Now he was just going to have to find a way to get him out.

CHAPTER TWELVE

BETH CAME AWAKE suddenly. She'd heard a sound in her room, but she didn't know for a moment if it was real or a dream.

Lying very still, she listened in the dark. She'd almost convinced herself the noise *had* sprung from a dream, when she heard it again. Someone was turning the doorknob, rattling it stealthily as if checking to see if it was locked.

Heart pounding, Beth rose up on her elbows, staring at the door. It was too dark to see if the knob was turning or not, but she'd definitely heard a sound.

As quietly as she could, she reached for the phone and dialed Clint's room number.

"Hello?" His voice was raspy with sleep.

"Clint." Her own voice was a frantic whisper. "I think someone is trying to get into my room."

The sleep instantly vanished from his voice. She could picture him catapulting out of bed. "Okay, listen to me. Lock yourself in the bathroom. I'll be right there."

Beth cradled the receiver with hardly a sound, then slipped out of bed and hurried into the bathroom. She locked herself in, then put her ear to the door to listen.

She couldn't hear anything, but her imagination was working in overdrive. She could see the door being forced open, someone bursting in....

"Beth?"

The sound of her name being softly called startled her.

"Beth? It's me. Let me in."

Releasing a breath of relief, she came out of the bathroom and hurried to the window, pulling back the curtain to peek out. "Clint?"

He stepped back so she could see him. "Open up."

She removed the chain lock and opened the door. "Did you see anything?" she asked anxiously.

He shook his head. "Whoever was here was gone by the time I got around the building. Are you okay?"

He stared at her so intently Beth shivered. "I'm fine. I was just so frightened when I heard the doorknob rattle. I was sure someone was trying to get in. I didn't know what else to do so I called you. Thank God you were here." She shivered again, and he pulled her into his arms, pressing her cheek against his shoulder. His lips skimmed her hair.

"I'm glad I'm here, too. Now," he said, easing slightly away, "tell me exactly what happened."

"A sound woke me up. It was very slight. I thought I'd been dreaming at first, but then I heard the doorknob rattle, like someone was testing to see if the door was locked. I don't think it was my imagination, Clint. I think someone really was outside my door."

His expression turned grim. "I'm going back out to have a look around in the parking lot. Lock the door behind me."

"Clint—" she caught his arm "—I don't think you should go. Whoever it was could have a weapon."

"I'll be careful." He stared down at her for a moment, his gaze hard, resolved. In the dim glow of light from the parking lot, she could see the definition of muscle in his arms and chest, the hard ripple of his abdomen where his jeans rode low. He looked suddenly very capable of taking care of a midnight intruder. Of taking care of her, for that matter.

After he was gone, Beth locked the door, then peeled back the heavy curtain to stare anxiously outside. But after Clint disappeared from her sight, nothing moved in the parking lot or out by the pool—not so much as a stray cat or a leaf blowing in the wind. The night was almost eerily silent. A light glowed inside the motel office, but Beth could see no movement from within. Where was Eddie? she wondered suddenly.

Clint came back a few minutes later, and she hurried to let him in. "Anything?"

He shook his head as he knelt and examined the door. "All you heard was a rattle?"

"Yes. And I had the chain lock fastened. I don't suppose whoever it was could have gotten in even if he'd managed to somehow disengage the lock."

Clint took another moment to study the door, then stood. "I don't see any marks on the lock or the frame. I don't think he tried to force his way in." He paused, frowning. "Are you sure the sound you heard wasn't a key being turned in the lock?"

Beth felt something go cold inside her. She caught her breath. "A key?"

Clint glanced at her. "A key that maybe hadn't been used in a long time. Or maybe a master key that had to be jiggled to work properly."

"Oh, my God," Beth blurted. "You don't really think it was Eddie, do you? I've had a feeling ever since I checked in that he's watching me."

"Why didn't you tell me?"

"Because I thought…" She paused. "I thought it would make me sound even more paranoid," she finished lamely.

"Paranoid or not, I think it's time I go have a little chat with Eddie." Clint's voice had hardened until Beth barely recognized it.

She felt chilled and excited at the same time. He was different here in Texas. Beth didn't know how to explain it, but in that instant she was very aware of the fact that he was shirtless and she wore nothing but a nightgown. She was very aware of the fact that she didn't want him to leave her side, even for a moment, and it had nothing to do with her fear.

She moistened her lips as she stared up at him. "I don't think talking to Eddie is a good idea. Even if he *was* the one trying to get into my room, we can't prove it. And besides…" she paused again. "I don't want you to leave."

He opened his mouth, as if to protest her argument, but then, seeing the look on her face, he stopped dead still. His gaze on her narrowed. "What do you mean, you don't want me to leave?"

"I want you to stay here tonight. With me." Oh, God. Had she really said that? Was she really, all of a sudden, that forward? What if he said no?

She heard the quick intake of his breath.

Their gazes met.

Slowly, Clint reached behind him and turned the bolt on the door. For good measure, he shoved home the chain lock as she'd done earlier, then turned back to face her. "Are you sure about this?"

"I…yes."

He cocked his head. "You don't sound all that sure, Beth."

"Well, then, maybe..." Her stomach fluttered with nerves. "Maybe you could do something to...convince me."

He moved toward her then, and in the blink of an eye, cupped the back of her neck with one hand. "And just how do you propose I do that?"

"You could start..."

"Yes?"

"You could start by kissing me. I really love the way you kiss, Clint."

He laughed softly. "You are full of surprises, aren't you?"

Some better than others, she thought, winding her arms around his neck. But she wouldn't dwell on the bad surprises that might be waiting for them in the morning.

Tonight was for the good surprises. And she had a feeling there would be several. She shivered as she pulled him to her.

WHERE WERE the reservations she'd had earlier? Clint wondered. Where was the woman who'd tried to send him away because she didn't want to hurt him? Who was so desperately afraid of her past?

Because the woman who stood before him now didn't seem afraid of anything. Not even an intruder who'd tried to break into her motel room.

That alone should have made Clint stop and reconsider what they were about to do, but she didn't give him a chance. She pressed herself against him until he had no choice but to respond, and his own doubts were suddenly history.

He couldn't think about anything but Beth, the way she kissed him, the way she plunged her hands into his hair. She seemed emboldened tonight, so sexy she was driving him crazy. She seemed…different.

Clint drew back for a moment, staring down into her upturned face. Her eyes…yes, those were the same. Large, luminous, violet-blue.

And her hair, the same.

Her lips…

Who are you? he thought in wonder.

More questions tried to intrude. That one-way ticket to Texas. Her reluctance to have him talk to Eddie.

Clint shoved them away. He wouldn't think about any of that now. He wouldn't think about anything but the way Beth made him feel. The way every inch of his body responded to her touch.

"What is it?" she murmured. "Why are you looking at me that way?" Her voice was the same, too. The soft timbre. The edge of self-doubt. He saw the old reluctance flicker back to life in her eyes, and he cursed inwardly, knowing he'd done that to her with his hesitation.

He lifted a hand to smooth back her hair. "Nothing's wrong. I just can't believe how beautiful you are."

She smiled. "I was afraid for a moment you were having second thoughts."

"Never." And even if he had been, he wasn't now. He could see in her eyes, in her face, everything he needed to know about her.

He wove his hands through her hair. "I love you," he whispered.

"I love you, too."

And in that moment, Clint knew that no matter

what they found out tomorrow, he would still love her. He wouldn't be able to help himself.

BETH HAD THOUGHT... For a moment she'd been so afraid....

But that fear was gone now. Clint loved her. Did anything else really matter? It would tomorrow. Lots of things would matter tomorrow. When they found out the truth about her past, it would *have* to matter. But tonight...

Tonight she would simply not think about tomorrow.

And then she wasn't able to think at all as Clint swept her up and carried her to bed. He lay down beside her and they kissed forever, deep, soul-shattering kisses that were thoroughly satisfying until the heat began to build unbearably and Clint's hands started to explore.

He pushed the straps of her nightgown down her arms, then slid the garment slowly from her body, taking his time, kissing her in places she'd never dreamed could be so sensual.

When he started to pull away, she clutched his shoulders. He kissed her again. "I'll be right back."

"Where—"

And then she realized that Clint had been thinking ahead whereas she'd been concerned only with the moment. He returned a few moments later and placed a foil-wrapped package on the nightstand while he slowly undressed.

Beth watched him, her blood racing with excitement. "Do you always travel so prepared?" she teased him.

"No, not always." His dark gaze never left hers. "Just when I'm chasing after a beautiful woman."

Beth's breath quickened. "And you do that often, do you? Chase after women?"

"Of course. At least once a decade."

He was undressed, and Beth could see the silhouette of his muscular body in the shadowy light. He was lean and hard and very masculine. Her heart started to pound as he moved over her.

"Now where were we?" he murmured.

"You were kissing me…"

"Right."

"And you were…" Beth placed his hand where she wanted it to be, and she heard Clint draw a sharp breath.

She arched her back, trembling as his mouth found hers and his hand…his hand touched her in ways Beth had only dreamed of.

She gasped as a fiery sensation shot through her body. "Clint, I don't think—"

"Don't think," he whispered, reaching for the condom.

Within seconds, he was inside her, moving slowly and deliberately at first. Then faster, harder…

Beth's head fell back against the pillow as something began to build inside her. Something exquisite and inevitable.

She plowed her fingers through his hair, pulling him toward her for a kiss that sent them both flying over the edge. Clint groaned against her mouth, shuddered as she shuddered, and then he kissed her again.

SHE HAD A HARD TIME facing him in the morning. Beth supposed a certain amount of awkwardness was inevitable in these kinds of situations, but deep down, she knew it wasn't their lovemaking that made her so uneasy. Today they would try to find a way to meet with Valerie Lake, and if she agreed to see them, they could learn Beth's true identity.

What would happen then?

What would happen if she turned out to be Rose Campbell, a thief, stalker and would-be murderer? Beth could go to jail for her crimes, but even if by some miracle she evaded prison, she and Clint would still be over. There was no way he could ever love a woman who'd done what Rose had done.

He rolled over, smiled and gave her a kiss. If he noticed her hesitation, he didn't comment. "As much as I'd like to spend the rest of the day right where we are, we should probably get moving. I'll go back to my room and shower. Give you some privacy." He kissed her again.

Beth ached to pull him back into her arms, to have him kiss her again and again until she was convinced that he would never leave her. But that wasn't possible and she knew it.

An hour later, he knocked on her door. It was a brilliant day outside. Sunlight glinted off the pool, temporarily blinding Beth as she drew back the door. She'd dressed for the weather, in slim white capris, a sleeveless cotton shirt and sandals.

Clint lifted his sunglasses briefly so that she could see his admiring stare. "You look...great."

"Thanks." Beth couldn't help but blush. The intimacy in his voice, the acknowledgment in his eyes that they were now lovers sent a thrill of awareness down her spine. He looked good, too, in jeans and a white T-shirt with the Twin Oaks logo over the left breast.

But he'd looked even better last night, she thought, as an image of their entwined bodies implanted itself in her mind.

"Are you blushing?" he teased as she stepped outside to join him.

"No, of course not. It was a little warm in my room, that's all." She fanned her face, as if to convince him.

"You were thinking about last night, weren't you? I've been thinking about it, too."

Beth could feel the heat rush up her neck and spread across her cheeks.

"And when you blush like that," he said, gazing down at her, "it reminds me of the way you looked when you—"

"Stop!" She put her hand on his chest. "I think maybe we shouldn't talk about last night."

He lifted a brow. "Why?"

"Because—"

"It embarrasses you?"

"No."

"Do you regret it?"

"No!"

"Good. Because I don't, either. Not one minute of it." He kissed her then, not passionately as he had the night before, but as if to let her know that it was the morning after and he still wasn't going anywhere.

"Should we go have breakfast and plot our strategy?" he asked when he finally drew away.

Beth nodded. "I think that might be a good idea. I have a rental car," she told him.

"So do I."

"Then you drive." Beth wasn't anxious to get back behind the wheel after the incident the evening before.

"I talked to Eddie," Clint informed her as they headed around the building to his car.

Beth turned in surprise. "When?"

"This morning after I left your room."

"What did he say?"

"Well, he didn't admit to trying to break into your room," Clint said dryly. "Not that I expected he would. He claims he didn't see anything suspicious, nor did he have complaints from any of the other guests."

"So he was on duty last night?"

"There's a night clerk that comes on duty at eleven, but according to Eddie, the guy's been out sick for a week. Eddie's been working his shift, too. Says he has a cot in a little room off the office that he catnaps on."

"Would this night clerk have access to the room keys?" Beth asked. "He might have a master key with him."

Clint shrugged. "Maybe. But I doubt we'd get any more out of him than I got out of Eddie."

They were in Clint's car by this time, and Beth glanced toward the office as they slowly drove by. "I still don't understand why he lied to me about knowing Valerie Lake."

"I asked him about that, too," Clint said. "He swears he doesn't remember her staying at the inn."

"Did you believe him?"

"I don't know. It's a little odd that he wouldn't at least remember her name, since she's living here now."

"Especially in a town this small," Beth insisted. "Everybody always knows everybody else's business. That's how it is in Cooper's Corner."

"Not quite." Clint slanted her a glance. "No one knew why you'd come to town. No one knew you had amnesia."

Okay, he had a point, Beth conceded. But she still found it doubtful that Eddie didn't know anything about Valerie Lake.

Beth directed Clint to the diner, and he pulled to the curb and parked. The tiny restaurant was more crowded than either of the other times Beth had been in. She and Clint found a booth, and a different waitress brought them water and menus.

"Is Darla working this morning?" Beth inquired politely.

"Yeah, but this is my station," the woman said a bit testily. Her gaze moved over them as if to assess her tip potential.

"I just need to talk to her for a moment," Beth explained. "Is she here?"

The waitress angled her head toward the kitchen. "She's helping out in the back. If I get a chance, I'll tell her she has company."

"Thanks."

They gave her their orders, and when she delivered the food several minutes later, she said, "Darla says to tell you she'll be out in a few minutes. I wouldn't count on it, though. We're pretty busy in here this morning, and the boss doesn't much like it when we socialize."

That hadn't stopped Darla before, but Beth merely smiled and thanked the woman for her trouble. She and Clint were nearly finished with breakfast before

Darla finally came out of the kitchen, wiping her hands on a dish towel. She walked over to the table with a smile.

"Well, hey there. You're getting to be a regular in here, aren't you?" She glanced at Clint. "And you brought a friend, I see."

"Clint Cooper." He half stood as he offered her his hand.

"Welcome to Mystique," she said. "We don't get many guys like you around here." She turned to Beth and winked. "Judy said you wanted to see me. What can I do for you?"

"You said your aunt works for Valerie Lake, right?" When Darla nodded, Beth said, as casually as she could, "Do you think she could get a message to Valerie for me? I drove out there yesterday, but the gate was locked and I didn't see an intercom. I called information, but they didn't have a listing for her. I'd really like to see her before I leave, but..." She shrugged, as if she didn't know what else to do.

"I guess it wouldn't hurt to call Aunt Birdie and ask her." Darla glanced over her shoulder. "My boss is kind of a jerk, though. He gets mad if we use the phone too much."

"You could try my cell," Clint offered. "I've been having trouble getting a signal here, though."

She eyed the tiny phone he offered her. "Nah, that's okay. Those things can cause brain tumors, you know? I'll just use the phone in the back. Boss says anything, I'll tell him I'm calling to check on a sick kid or something."

Darla hurried off and came back a moment later with a message from her aunt. "She's going out there this afternoon, but she said it wouldn't do you any good to try and see Valerie while she's working. She won't take calls or anything. But Aunt Birdie said if you just happened to coincidentally be out by the gate—'' she winked at Beth ''—when she leaves at six, she'll go back and tell Valerie you want to see her. She can't guarantee that Valerie will agree, though.''

"I understand. Thanks so much for your help, Darla."

"Yes, thank you," Clint echoed. He left a tip on the table and then went up to the register to pay the check. Beth suspected he would make sure Darla got a healthy tip, as well.

Outside, he put on his sunglasses and slipped an arm around Beth's shoulders. "Sure you want to do this?"

"I don't think I have a choice, Clint."

"I guess not." He seemed to stare off into space for a moment, and then his gaze settled on her. She couldn't see his eyes behind the dark glasses, but she felt a thrill slide over her just the same. "We've got a lot of time to kill before six, and we've got the car with us. Want to do some sightseeing?"

"No," she said slowly. "What I'd really like to do is go back to the motel."

"BETH...Beth..."

She closed her eyes at the sound of his voice. How could the mere whisper of her name do such intense things to her insides? How could his hands, his mouth, his body make her every nerve ending scream for release?

Last night had been a slow exploration of new territory, but today...today was a frenzied coupling that had them tearing at each other's clothing the moment the door to Clint's room closed behind them.

They kissed all the way across the floor to the bathroom, where Clint grabbed a condom from his travel kit. Then they fell on the bed, arms and legs entwined, their bodies becoming one almost instantly. They lay side by side, face-to-face, Beth's leg slung over Clint's hip as he rocked frantically against her. Her back arched, her head rolled back, and she gasped as his mouth pressed against the pulse point in her throat.

This time, their passion was anything but restrained. They couldn't kiss long enough. Couldn't move fast or hard enough. And yet when the explosion came, when shudder after shudder racked Beth's body, the ferocity of her climax shocked her. How could the human body withstand such a sensual assault…and still want more?

They lay as they were before, arms and legs still tangled, bodies still joined and trembling from the aftershock.

Beth lifted her head. "Clint—"

"Shush." His head had fallen back against the pillows, and his eyes were tightly closed. "Don't say anything. Not yet."

She understood. After what they'd just done to each other, with each other, for each other…what really was there to say?

CHAPTER THIRTEEN

"I'M SORRY TO KEEP YOU waiting," Darla's aunt said with a shrug. She was a short, heavyset woman with a rugged, careworn face and flinty eyes. She looked as if she was well into her sixties, but Beth thought she was the kind of woman who had probably worked hard all her life and had no illusions or expectations of a cushy retirement.

They had been waiting for her at the gate when she pulled up on the other side, and then had walked over and introduced themselves.

"Now, I told Darla to tell you that I can't make no promises," she warned them. She glanced over her shoulder at the house. "Valerie is a might on the peculiar side. She don't much like to socialize, and she sure don't want no one interrupting her while she's working."

Having said that, the older woman promised to do her best. "Let me see if I got it right," she said with a frown. "You've got some information about someone named Rose Campbell that she might be interested in. That's the message, right?"

Beth nodded, her heart in her throat. "Yes."

Birdie gave them a curt nod, threw her ancient Buick into reverse and backed up the driveway in a cloud of dust.

Beth and Clint walked back to their own car to wait. Five minutes later, the Buick appeared again. This time the gates swung open, and Birdie drove through. She pulled alongside their car and rolled down her window as the gates closed behind her.

"She says she's going to be working most of the night. Doesn't want to be disturbed."

Beth didn't know whether to be relieved or crushed. She'd been on such an emotional roller coaster for days now that a part of her just wanted to get it over with. Find out once and for all if she had a connection to Valerie Lake and Rose Campbell. Then maybe she could find a way to deal with it.

But this limbo was excruciating. The knowledge that her past could tear her and Clint apart at any moment was almost unbearable.

Clint leaned across Beth to speak out the window. "Did she say when there might be a better time to see her?"

Birdie shook her gray head. "No. I told her what you said. About that Rose person, I mean. To tell you the truth, she didn't seem that interested. If you want my opinion, I think you're wasting your time."

"HOW COULD SHE NOT BE interested?" Beth asked on the way back to town. She stared out the window, feeling numb and curiously detached. Maybe that was a defense mechanism, she decided. A way to cope with all the highs and lows she was being put through.

"I don't know." Clint's voice sounded grim, determined. Maybe even a little angry. "But I don't think we should give up. There's got to be a way to get her to see us."

That was another thing that was starting to bother Beth again—Clint's determination to be by her side when she talked to Valerie. She was glad that he was with her, glad they'd made love—she could never regret that—but she still wasn't certain she wanted him present when she talked to Valerie. It would be easier to face the truth if she didn't have to see Clint's face when and if her worst fears came true. If she really was Rose Campbell.

Maybe it would be best if she convinced him to go back to Cooper's Corner, Beth mused. Maybe she should just go back there, too. Then later, in a few weeks, she could return here quietly on her own.

"What the hell—"

Clint's curse broke into her thoughts as the car swerved violently toward the shoulder. A pickup truck with yellow flames painted across the hood had taken a curve at a dangerous speed and momentarily lost control, careening for one split second across the centerline toward them.

The truck blazed by them in a cloud of dust, and Beth turned, watching it disappear down the road.

"Idiot," Clint muttered.

"I think I've seen that truck before. At the motel."

He shot her a glance. "Are you sure?"

"Unless there's more than one with the same paint job," Beth said, "I think it might be Eddie's."

"Let's find out where he's going." Clint whipped the car around and headed back toward Valerie's house, but the truck was nowhere in sight. If he'd turned into Valerie's drive, the dust had already settled. There was nothing to indicate she'd had a recent visitor.

WHEN THEY GOT BACK to the motel, the first thing Clint did was walk over to the office to see if Eddie was around. A man he'd never seen before sauntered out of the back when he rang the bell.

"What can I do you for?" the man asked in a heavy drawl. He was taller and younger than Eddie, but he had the same eyes, the same build, the same lazy mannerisms.

"Is Eddie around?"

"Nah, he had some errands to run. I'm Del Ray, his nephew."

"Do you know when Eddie will be back?" Clint asked.

Del Ray scratched his arm as he peered across the counter at Clint. "Anything I can help you with?"

"No, I just need to see Eddie about something," Clint answered evasively.

Evidently, Del Ray was a lot sharper than he looked. His gaze narrowed suspiciously. "He went to see his mother. She's been down and out with her back lately. Don't know when he'll return."

"Does she live out by the old sawmill?" Clint asked casually.

Something sparked in Del Ray's eyes. "Why do you ask?"

"I thought I saw Eddie's truck out there earlier."

"Out by the sawmill?" Del Ray gave a nervous bark of laughter. "No, sir, it weren't Eddie you saw. I guarantee it weren't Eddie. He wouldn't be caught dead out by that place. Not with dark coming. Besides, his mother lives on the other side of town."

Clint had no idea what to make of the man's adamant denial. "Well," he said. "I guess I must have been mistaken. Is there someone else in town who drives a truck similar to Eddie's?''

But Del Ray just shook his head. ''Hey, you got any more questions, maybe you better wait and ask my uncle.''

As soon as Clint got back to his room, he put in a call to Maureen. She answered on the first ring, sounding frantic. ''Where on earth have you been?'' she all but shouted. ''I've been trying to reach you for hours. Why didn't you return my calls?''

''What calls? Maureen, what's wrong? What's happened? Is it Keegan?''

''Yes, it's Keegan. But he's okay,'' she rushed to assure him. ''At least, I think he is.''

Clint's heart started to pound. ''What do you mean, you think he is?''

Maureen hesitated. ''Maybe you'd better sit down.''

''Just tell me, damn it. You're scaring the hell out of me.''

''Clint, I think he's in Texas.''

''What!'' Clint dropped down on the edge of the bed.

''I think he must have overheard our phone conversation last night,'' Maureen was saying. ''He thinks you and Beth are in danger, and he figures it's all his fault. Clint, I he's think coming to try and rescue you.''

Clint swore viciously. ''Do you have any idea where he is right now, at this very moment?''

''No, not really. We know he took a bus to Boston late last night.''

"Last night!"

"I know, I know, I feel terrible. It's all my fault. He told me he was spending the night with Bryan. I didn't think anything of it. But Bryan got scared and told his mother. She called me and I've been trying to reach you ever since. Your cell phone doesn't work, the operator says you're out of the service area or something, and you didn't return the messages I left at the motel."

"I never got any messages." He swore again.

"Well, never mind that now. We're on top of things from this end. I've had Quigg pull some strings. Keegan used your credit card number to book a flight online. We know he flew out of Logan before lunch, with a connection in Dallas. His flight got into Austin just after three."

"It's almost seven." Clint's mind was racing. What would Keegan's next move have been once he reached Austin? He was only thirteen, so he couldn't rent a car. Doubtful he'd have the money to take a cab all the way to Mystique. "Have you checked the bus terminal in Austin?"

"We're working on that now," Maureen told him. "There's a lot of red tape to cut through when it comes to passenger manifests these days."

Clint barely heard her. He was wondering if he should drive to Austin right now and look for his son himself. Austin was a small city, but it was still plenty big enough for a boy to get lost in.

"We know Keegan's final destination is Mystique," Maureen said. "I've checked the bus schedules from Austin. There's a Greyhound due in at seven-thirty. Chances are if he's not already there, he'll be on that one. Find out where the bus stops, then get over there and wait for him."

They hung up and Clint headed for the door. He drove around the building to Beth's room, and got out to knock on her door.

She answered, looking anxious. "Clint! Is...everything okay?"

"I just talked to Maureen. She told me Keegan's on his way here."

Beth put a hand to her throat. "On his way here? But...how? Why?"

Clint shrugged. "He's got some notion that all this is his fault. I guess he's coming here to try and make things right."

"*His* fault? But that's ridiculous." Beth's eyes glittered with tears. "He has nothing to do with this."

"We know that, but I guess he doesn't." Clint paused. "It was the same when Kristin died. He blamed himself because the two of them had an argument that morning. He didn't get over his guilt for a long time, and I think that's why he got into so much trouble. But that's all water under the bridge now. I just want to find him and make sure he's all right."

Beth touched his arm. "What are you going to do?"

"Maureen says there's a bus due in town at seven-thirty. I'm going to find out where it stops and wait for him."

"I know where the bus stops," Beth said suddenly. "I saw the sign yesterday. It's down the street from the diner."

"You're sure about that?"

"I'm positive." When he started to turn away, she grabbed his arm. "Clint, is there anything I can do? Do you want me to come with you?"

"No. It's probably better if you stay here. If he's not on the bus, he might try to call. I'll stop by the office and tell them to transfer my calls to your room."

"Clint..." Her hand tightened on his arm. "I'm sure he's okay. He's very intelligent, and from what you've told me, he's pretty street savvy as well."

"Yeah." But he was only thirteen, Clint thought. And at that age, street smarts could sometimes get you into big trouble.

BETH WATCHED CLINT'S CAR pull away from the motel and merge with the meager traffic on Main Street. Within moments he was out of sight, and she started to pace, wringing her hands in agitation. She'd wanted to tell him about the phone call she'd gotten just moments before he knocked on her door, but after hearing about Keegan and seeing the worry on Clint's face, she knew it wasn't the right time. Her problems could wait. Finding Keegan safe and sound was the only thing that mattered.

But as worried as she was about Keegan, she couldn't stop thinking about that call. "Is this Beth Young?" a female voice had asked her.

"Yes." Something about the woman's tone had made the hair stand up on the back of Beth's neck.

"I'm Valerie Lake. I understand you want to see me."

Beth's heart started to pound. "But I didn't leave

my name this afternoon. How did you know who I was? How did you know where to find me?''

"This is a very small town, Ms. Young. A few phone calls is usually all it takes to find out anything you need to." She paused. "My housekeeper said you had information about a woman named Rose Campbell.''

"Do you know her?" Beth asked anxiously.

"I used to. But Rose Campbell is dead."

Shock surged through Beth, leaving her trembling as she clutched the phone. "Are you sure? When?"

"Rose Campbell is not a subject I particularly care to discuss," the woman said tersely. "What exactly is the nature of the information you have about her?''

Beth hesitated, her mind racing. "If Rose is dead, I'm not sure it matters.''

"I guess this call was a waste of my time, then.''

"No, wait." Beth tried to think what to do. This woman was the only clue she had to her past. She couldn't let her go. Not yet. "Would it be possible for us to still meet?''

"Why?"

Beth swallowed. "I know this is going to sound strange, but I was in a car accident two years ago, in San Bernardino County in California. My car went over the side of a mountain. I was in a coma for a while, and when I woke up, my memory was gone. I don't know who I am or where I'm from. I don't know anything about my past life.''

"How does this have anything to do with me?" The woman's tone was blunt, uninterested.

"Maybe nothing," Beth conceded. "But I have

reason to believe there could be a connection between us. I think you may know me.''

There was silence for a long moment, then the woman said very softly, ''You're mistaken.''

''How can you be so sure until you see me? When did you compose 'After the Rain'?''

''I don't see how that's any of your business.'' Was that a note of panic in the woman's voice?

''I've been playing that song for two years,'' Beth said. ''Ever since I came out of my coma.''

By now, Beth's heart was pounding so hard she thought the woman on the other end must surely hear it. Then, very softly, Valerie Lake said, ''If you know what's good for you, you'll never play that song again. You'll get in your car and go back to wherever you came from. If you try to make trouble for me, I promise you you'll be very, very sorry. 'After the Rain' is my song. Do you hear me? It's *mine!*''

The connection had been severed then, and Beth had stood for a moment, shivering in the aftermath of the woman's rage.

She wanted desperately to talk to Clint about the phone call, but that conversation would have to come later, when they knew Keegan was safe.

BETH WAS STILL PACING her room a few minutes later when the phone rang. Wondering if it might be Valerie again, she hesitated to answer it. Even over the telephone, the woman had made a strong impression on her, one she couldn't seem to shake. Beth hated to admit it, but Valerie Lake had frightened her.

She thought of Clint's theory that the woman living in Mystique was actually Rose Campbell, and the idea no longer seemed so preposterous. Not after having talked to the woman, hearing her voice...

Beth stared at the phone for another long moment, then, thinking the call might be from Keegan or Clint, she hurried over to answer it. "Hello?"

"Miss Young?" A male voice this time.

Beth let out a breath she hadn't realized she'd been holding. "Yes?"

"This is Eddie, over at the office. I've got a young man here says his name's Keegan Cooper. He's looking for his dad, but Mr. Cooper isn't in his room. He left a little while ago. You have any idea where we can find him?"

Beth's heart knocked excitedly. "Keegan's in the office with you right now?"

"Yes, ma'am. Good-looking young fellow. Brown hair, green eyes. Looks like his dad."

"Just have him wait for me," Beth said. "I'll be right there."

She glanced at her watch. It wasn't yet seven-thirty. Clint would still be at the bus stop waiting. She and Keegan could drive over there and surprise him.

Hurrying into the office a few moments later, Beth anxiously glanced around. No one was there.

But...she'd asked Eddie to keep Keegan in the office. She hadn't been more than a couple of minutes crossing the parking lot. No way she could have missed them.

"Eddie?" She rang the bell on the counter. "Eddie! Keegan?"

Nothing but silence. She started to turn back to the door when a sound that might have been a whimper came from the back room.

"Eddie? Keegan?"

Beth walked around the counter and glanced through the doorway. The room was dark. Her eyes took a moment to adjust, and even then she could only make out vague shapes. A desk. A cot shoved against one wall.

"Keegan? Are you in here?"

"No, ma'am, he's not," a voice said behind her.

Beth whirled as something hard crashed against her skull. Her knees buckled, and just before she hit the floor, she heard a man drawl, "But don't you worry none. I'm fixing to take you to him."

THE BUS WAS ALMOST an hour late, and when it finally lumbered to a stop at the curb, only two passengers disembarked and neither of them was Keegan. After the driver had retrieved their bags from the luggage hold, Clint approached him.

"My son was supposed to be on this bus," he explained. "He's thirteen years old, tall, slim, brown hair. Do you remember seeing him? Did he get off at another stop?"

The driver shook his head. "He didn't get on my bus."

"You're sure?"

"I'm positive. I make a point to look at each and every passenger that gets on, just in case I ever need to give a description to the police. You never know in this day and age. Nobody matching the description you gave me got on my bus."

"Okay," Clint said. "I believe you. But...do you mind if I have look for myself? Just to be sure. He might be asleep and missed his stop."

"Nobody's allowed on without a ticket."

"Then you go look. Please," Clint insisted. "We're talking about my boy here."

The driver's face softened, and he nodded. He came back a few minutes later with the same verdict. "He's not on there."

Clint sighed. "Thanks anyway."

"No problem. I hope you find him soon."

"Thanks."

Clint walked back to his car and got in. Taking out his cell phone, he tried to call Maureen, but he still couldn't get a signal. Cursing his wireless company, he tossed the phone on the seat and beat a fist against the steering wheel. "Keegan," he muttered. "Where the hell are you, Son?"

There was nothing he could do but go back to the motel and call Maureen. Maybe she'd found out something since they'd last talked. At the very least, she could get Quigg to pull some more strings and have the Austin police start looking.

When he drove up to the motel, he saw the black truck with the yellow flames parked near the office. Clint got out and went inside. Eddie was standing at the counter, flipping through a magazine. He looked up when Clint walked in, and nodded.

"Hey," he said. "You find your boy?"

"What do you know about my son?" Clint asked sharply.

"Take it easy," Eddie said. "Del Ray told me you came in asking to have your calls transferred to Ms. Young's room in case your boy called. Then right after you left, he came in."

Clint's heart lurched. "Are you sure it was Keegan?"

"Told me his name clear as a bell. I called Ms. Young's room, and she came over and got him."

"Did they go back to her room? I didn't see her car in the parking lot."

"That's because she and the boy took off after she came and got him. I figured they were going to find you."

"Which direction were they headed?" Clint asked anxiously.

"South, toward the freeway. Come to think of it, something did strike me a little odd about the situation. Wherever they were headed, she sure seemed in a great big hurry to get there. She was breaking all kinds of speed limits."

Clint's first reaction was intense relief that Keegan was okay and he was with Beth. But where in the hell had they gone off to in such a hurry? Beth knew Clint was at the bus stop waiting for Keegan. She knew he was worried sick about his son. Why hadn't she brought Keegan to him?

Clint's gaze narrowed on Eddie. Something wasn't right here. "My sister's been trying to reach me all day. Her name's Maureen Cooper. She said she left several messages at the desk. Can you explain to me why I never got any of them?"

Eddie scratched his head. "Well, now, that is peculiar, but maybe you should ask your friend about it when you catch up with her. Because I called your room and gave her the messages. She said she'd pass them along to you."

Clint's gaze narrowed on the man. "That's not possible. Beth and I were together all day. I would have known if you'd called.''

Eddie shrugged. "I don't know what to tell you then. Someone answered the phone in your room. A woman. I gave her the messages and she said she'd give them to you. If it wasn't Miss Young, I don't know who it was.''

He was lying, Clint thought angrily, and for a moment, the urge to grab Eddie by his shirt and haul him across the counter was almost irresistible. The rage and fear surging through Clint's veins might have made him do exactly that, but then something occurred to him. He and Beth *hadn't* been together all day. Earlier, when they'd been in his room, he'd stepped outside to the vending machines. He wouldn't have heard the phone while he was outside, or later, when he was in the shower. Was it possible Eddie had called during one of those times? But if he'd given Beth the messages, why wouldn't she have told him?

He turned back to Eddie. "Why do I get the feeling you're lying to me? You know something about this, don't you?''

Eddie threw up his hands. "Now, why in the hell would I lie about something like that? Looky here, if you and your lady friend are going to cause me this much trouble, maybe you both better just pack up and leave. I don't need this kind of grief. Be out of here in an hour, both of you.''

"All right," Clint said. "We'll do just that. But you wouldn't mind having a chat with the sheriff before I go, would you? I'd like you to tell him everything you've told me.''

A flash of emotion that Clint couldn't name flickered across Eddie's features before he gave a careless shrug. "I wouldn't mind a bit. The sheriff's a personal friend of mine. You just go ahead and get him if you've a mind to." He smiled, but his eyes had gone cold and hard, making Clint think that in spite of his laid-back demeanor, Eddie Barksdale could probably be a pretty nasty customer if crossed.

Realizing he wasn't apt to get anything out of the man, Clint shoved open the office door and stepped outside, his gaze scanning the parking lot. Beth's car was still missing.

He hurried over and knocked on her door. It creaked open, and Clint stepped inside. He noticed immediately that the closet was empty and her suitcase was gone. Striding over to the bathroom, he flipped on the light. Her toiletries were missing, too. The room was empty.

What the hell was going on? Where was Beth? Where had she taken Keegan?

He picked up the phone and called Maureen. "Clint," she said in relief when she heard his voice. "I've been going crazy here. Did you find him? Was he on the bus?"

"No, he wasn't on the bus, and something really weird is going on here." Quickly, he related everything Eddie had told him.

"You say her things are gone from her room?"

"Yes," Clint said, fighting off a momentary panic. *Where had she taken Keegan?* "But there's no way she and Keegan would have left without letting me know. Not unless the two of them were in some kind of trouble."

"And this Eddie person said it looked as if she was in a big hurry?"

"Yes. He said they were headed toward the freeway, but I don't trust the guy. I'm not convinced he wasn't the one who tried to break into Beth's room. And I don't believe for a minute he gave her your messages. He's up to something, Maureen. I'd bet you anything he's the reason Beth and Keegan are missing."

"Okay, calm down," his sister advised. "Don't jump to any conclusions until you know for sure what you're dealing with. Are you absolutely positive someone tried to break into Beth's room? You said there was no evidence. You didn't see anyone fleeing the scene."

"That doesn't mean it didn't happen."

"I know that, but…" She trailed off. "I keep going over and over this whole thing in my mind. What if Beth really is Rose Campbell? She stalked Valerie Lake and tried to kill her. What if she's turned her sick obsession on you? And on Keegan? I've seen it happen, Clint. People who are that troubled are sometimes capable of just about anything."

A cold chill settled over Clint. "Beth is not like that. She isn't capable of violence."

"But you don't know that for sure, do you?"

"I know *her*."

"The woman you know doesn't really exist," Maureen reminded him gently. "I may be all wrong about this. I hope I am wrong. I like Beth. I wanted the two of you to get together. If she is capable of the behavior I just described, then she fooled me, too. But what we have to concentrate on now is finding

Keegan. We can't leave any stone unturned. I'll have Quigg alert the Texas DPS and the Austin PD to be on the lookout, and right now, I need you to go back over and get her license plate number from this Eddie person. Most motels require it on the registration card. When you have it, call me back." Maureen paused. "Try not to panic, Clint. We'll find him, I promise."

"I know. And thanks."

"Get me that number." Her voice was brisk again, the consummate professional. Whatever emotion she was feeling, she managed to hide it. "We can track it down through the rental agency if we have to, but this will make things a lot easier—"

"Hold on a minute," Clint interrupted. He'd been staring absently out the window as Maureen spoke, but now he saw something that caught his attention. Eddie was hurrying out to his truck.

Clint tossed the phone to the bed and ran out of the room, waving his arms and shouting for Eddie to stop, but if the man saw him, he pretended not to. He shot out of the motel drive and headed toward downtown. Clint kept running until he was at the office door, and when he found it locked, he gave it a vicious shake.

Beth's registration card was locked inside, along with the license plate number of her rental car.

He started back to the room, then paused, backtracking when he noticed a residue on the pavement where Eddie's truck had been parked. He squatted and ran his finger through the debris. Sawdust.

It must have fallen out of the tread in the tires. Where would you go to drive through sawdust?

Out by the sawmill? No, sir, it weren't Eddie you

saw. I guarantee it weren't Eddie. He wouldn't be caught dead out by that place.

Clint had thought at the time that Del Ray's protests were a bit vociferous, but he'd later forgotten about it. The conversation came back to him now, and in a flash, Clint was up and running for Beth's room. He grabbed the receiver off the bed. "Maureen?"

"What the devil is going on, Clint? Where'd you go?"

"I think I know where they've been taken."

"You mean Keegan?"

"I mean Keegan and Beth. They've both been kidnapped, and I think I've just figured out where they are. There's an old abandoned sawmill a mile or so north of town. I'd bet my life that's where they are."

The problem was, he was betting on Keegan's and Beth's lives as well. But Clint wouldn't let himself think about that. Wouldn't let himself dwell on the possibility that he could be wrong and they could be wasting precious time.

"Okay, it's time to call in the locals," Maureen said with steely resolve.

"Yes, call them," Clint said. "Tell them I'm headed out to the old sawmill."

"Clint, wait a second! You can't go tearing off without backup. You aren't even armed. Wait for the police—"

He threw the phone down and ran.

CHAPTER FOURTEEN

WHEN BETH CAME TO, her head throbbed with pain. Groaning, she tried to lift her hand to the spot where she'd been hit, but the effort was too great. She squeezed her eyes closed and willed the darkness to descend again, but a voice kept calling her back.

"Miss Young? Beth? Wake up!"

Her eyes fluttered open. She could barely make out the outline of someone bending over her. Everything was still so hazy.

"Miss Young?"

"Keegan?" She tried to shake off her grogginess, tried to focus.

"You're not dead," he said in relief. "I'm glad."

"Me, too." She pushed herself up on her elbows. The pain in her head threatened to flatten her again, but she gritted her teeth and tried to ignore it. "Where are we?"

"Some kind of toolshed, I think. But there's nothing in here we can use to get out. I already looked." Keegan's voice sounded anxious and frightened, but he was trying very hard not to show it.

Beth's gaze drifted upward to where dim light filtered in. "Is there a window up there?"

"Too high to reach, and too small to fit through. I already tried that, too."

Beth was sitting up now, gazing around at their shadowy prison. ''Do you have any idea where this shed is located?''

''It's in an old mill or something. It was daylight when they brought me out here.'' His voice dropped ominously. ''They didn't blindfold me or anything.''

It took a moment for the portent of his words to sink in. Then Beth went cold with fear. They'd brought him here in daylight without a blindfold, not caring that he'd seen his surroundings, because they didn't intend for either of them to get out alive.

Beth tried to beat back her panic. She knew she had to remain calm and rational for Keegan's sake. She had to find a way to get them out of there. ''Do you know who brought us here? And why?''

Keegan lifted his shoulders. ''I don't know why, but that guy from the motel brought me out here. He said he was taking me to my dad.''

''You mean Eddie?''

''Yeah, I think so. Tall. Skinny. Wears a cowboy hat.''

''That sounds like him.''

''I heard him talking to a woman. They said something about someone named Del Ray driving your car back to Austin for the police to find. So I guess there's at least three of them in on it.''

But what exactly was ''it''? Beth tried to digest everything Keegan had told her, but none of it made much sense. Why had Eddie Barksdale and a man named Del Ray kidnapped her and Keegan? For ransom? And who was the woman Keegan had heard talking to Eddie?

"Do you think you can help me up, Keegan? We've got to find a way out of here—"

The door opened suddenly, and a female voice said coldly, "Get up, both of you. It's time to go."

Beth knew the voice instantly. It was the woman who'd phoned her only a short while ago. "Where are you taking us?" she demanded, trying to sound strong and capable even though her insides were quivering with terror.

"Just get up," the woman ordered, "if you know what's good for you."

She stood silhouetted in the doorway, and something glinted in her hand. A gun, Beth thought with a shiver. Dear God, she had to get Keegan out of here. She had to get him safely back to Clint.

Clint…

No, she wouldn't think about him now. She wouldn't let herself dwell on the possibility she might never see him again.

She staggered to her feet, and Keegan took her arm to help steady her. The woman who called herself Valerie Lake stepped back so they could walk through the door, and as Beth passed by her, she said, "You look different."

Beth caught her breath. "You…do know me then." Was she Rose? Was she the real Valerie? All of Clint's suppositions came flooding back to Beth, and for a moment she could do nothing but stare at the woman helplessly. She alone held the key to Beth's past. "Who am I?" she asked in a tortured whisper.

But the woman just laughed. "Where you're going, you won't need to know." She gestured with the gun.

"Start walking. Over that way. I'll tell you when to stop."

They headed toward the far side of the mill, and as they walked along, Beth frantically glanced around for some means of escape, some way to protect Keegan. Piles of rotting lumber dotted the landscape, providing cover, and boards strewn along the ground were potential weapons. But how could she pick one up without the woman seeing her? If she could somehow create a diversion, Beth thought a little desperately, maybe Keegan could get away. He could hide behind the stacks of lumber until help came.

If help came. Who would even think to look for them here?

After a few moments, the giant piles of sawdust loomed ahead of them in the dusk, reminding Beth of Egyptian pyramids. An earthy, decayed scent permeated the air, and she thought with a shiver of the young man who'd lost his life inside one of those gargantuan mounds.

As she gazed at the small mountains, she suddenly knew why they'd been brought here. No one ever came to the sawmill, Darla had said. The sawdust piles were a perfect place to hide dead bodies.

Beth's stomach churned with fear. She glanced over her shoulder. The woman was right behind them.

"What do you want from us?" Beth tried to keep her voice steady and strong, but it was difficult when she knew that in a few short minutes both she and Keegan would be dead if she didn't think of some way out of this.

"I don't want much," the woman said with a shrug. "Just your silence."

Beth turned slightly toward her. "Our silence about what?"

She gestured absently with the gun. "I have to make sure you don't repeat to anyone else what you said to me on the phone today."

Beth stopped and turned. "What did I say?"

The woman halted as well, and for a moment, Beth was afraid she'd made a fatal mistake. That instead of buying them time, she'd tried the woman's patience, and she'd just shoot them on the spot.

But to Beth's surprise, the woman answered her. "You said you'd been playing 'After the Rain' ever since you woke up from your coma. That song was released only two weeks ago, on the same day the movie came out. If the right people—or should I say the wrong people—got wind of your allegation, they might start asking questions."

Oh, my God. The woman before her really was Rose then. A stalker. A would-be murderer. And Beth was—

"You don't need Keegan," she said desperately. "He doesn't even know what you're talking about. Let him go," she pleaded.

The woman slowly shook her head. "I can't do that. I *do* need him. I need him to convince everyone how crazy you really are...Rose."

At the sound of Beth's gasp, Keegan spun to face their tormentor. "I won't tell anyone anything," he said fiercely. "Not about Beth. You can just forget about that."

The woman made an impatient sound. "All right, enough of this. Turn around and keep walking. And don't worry, little man. You won't need to say a word. Your disappearance will say it all." Her voice took on a dramatic timbre. "A disturbed woman with a record of stalking and attempted murder pretends to have amnesia in order to get close to a handsome widower and his son, but when the widower starts to suspect her true identity, she grabs the son and disappears with him. Nobody ever sees them again. It would be just like something Rose Campbell would do. Right?"

Beth felt sick to her stomach. Her knees trembled with fear. With horror. "On the phone, you said Rose was dead," she whispered.

"Oh, she is. She's been dead for over two years."

Beth turned in confusion. *"What?"*

The woman motioned with the gun. "Did I tell you to stop? I *said* keep walking. You go on like this and I'll have to shoot you right here. And then the boy will have to drag your body the rest of the way. Is that what you want?"

Beth put out her hand in supplication. It was shaking badly, but she hoped the woman wouldn't notice. "Please. Just tell me about…Rose. How can she be dead?" Wasn't *she* Rose? Wasn't that what the woman had implied? "How can she have been dead for over two years when she broke into Valerie Lake's house two years ago."

"Did she?"

The woman's smile chilled Beth's blood. "I… don't understand."

"You don't have to understand. In a matter of seconds, none of this is going to matter to you in the least."

"Please," Beth whispered. "Just tell me what happened. What difference can it make to you?'' *Please, God, let me keep her talking until I can find a way out of this.*

The woman's voice went icy with scorn. ''Please this and please that,'' she mimicked. ''Buying time isn't going to prevent the inevitable.''

''I know, I know,'' Beth said quickly. She took a deep breath, trying to calm her nerves. ''It's just all so confusing. Please tell me about Rose.''

''Why do you keep mentioning her name?'' the woman shouted with sudden fury. ''I don't want to talk about her! Don't you understand anything? That woman was a parasite who tried to latch on to my life. I'm glad she's dead. The world is well rid of her.''

''Then—'' Beth stopped abruptly, her mind reeling in confusion. Who was who here? Was Rose Campbell really dead? And if so, did that mean the woman who stood before them was the real Valerie Lake? Where did that leave Beth? Was she not connected to either one of them? Was all this for *nothing?*

Concentrate, she warned herself. None of that mattered right now. She had to keep her wits about her. She had to somehow keep ''Valerie'' talking until she and Keegan could find a way to escape.

''Rose was obsessed with you, wasn't she? She stalked you. That must have been terrifying for you.'' Beth's heart was pounding against her rib cage like the wings of a trapped bird, but she tried to keep her voice calm, nonthreatening. Maybe even a little sympathetic. After all, if this woman was the real Valerie Lake, then she'd been a recluse for years. She needed to talk. Needed to get it all out, confess her sins to someone who would never be able to repeat them.

Just keep her talking, Beth coached herself. *Oh, God, please let me be able to keep her talking.*

Valerie's laugh was cold and brittle. "Do you really think the sympathetic act is going to work?" She took a step toward Beth and Keegan, the hand that held the gun frighteningly steady. "I assure you it won't, so let's just get this over with."

"No, wait!" Beth cast a frantic glance at Keegan, wondering what must be going through his head. He was so quiet. Was he as frightened as she was? "How did Rose die?"

Valerie paused. A look went across her face that turned Beth's blood to ice. And just like that, she knew.

"You killed her, didn't you?" Beth said in horror.

Valerie cocked her head. "Now, all of a sudden, I'm not so sure you do have amnesia."

"I do," Beth said. "But think about it for a minute. If I figured it out, someone else will, too."

Valerie shook her head. "No one will. And if they do, they won't be able to prove anything. I'll cover my tracks, just like I did before."

"But…you didn't cover them, did you? You meant to kill me on that mountain. But I'm alive and I came looking for you. And if you kill us, someone else will come looking for you. Someone will always be looking for you."

Valerie's hand wasn't so steady now as she aimed the gun at Beth's heart. "I won't make the same mistake twice. This time, you *will* die."

Beth's mouth went completely dry with fear, but

somehow she managed to croak, "Just tell me my name before I die. Give me that, at least."

Valerie wavered, as if unsure whether to grant her a last wish or not, but then she shrugged. "Your name is Annie Lockhart. You were my assistant."

And in a flash of blinding pain, Beth knew that it was true. Knew that she *was* Annie Lockhart. "Oh, my God..." She put both hands to her head, dropping to her knees at the excruciating pain behind her eyelids. Somewhere in the deep recesses of her mind, she heard music. *Her* music. "After the Rain" was her song. It meant something intensely personal to her. She'd written that song in the throes of grief. She didn't know how she knew this, but she did.

She looked up, the pain still throbbing behind her eyelids. "You stole my song," she blurted. "You stole 'After the Rain.' That's why you tried to kill me." She hadn't realized that Keegan had dropped to his knees beside her, but now she felt his arm tighten around her shoulders.

A strange look came over Valerie's features. "It was the most beautiful song I'd ever heard," she said softly, reverently. "You were playing it in the music room one day, and you didn't hear me come in. I stood in the doorway, listening to you play. The music flowed so effortlessly from your fingertips. The song was so beautiful, so...gut-wrenching. It was the kind of song I used to write.

"When you were finished, I asked you about it, and you just shrugged it off. It was just something you'd written after your mother died, you said. Something to help you through your grief. It was nothing.

"Nothing! I would have sold my soul to have written that song! It represented *everything* to me. When I asked if you'd ever considered finding a market for it, you just laughed at me. 'Oh, I couldn't take money for something so personal,'" she chanted in a sickeningly sweet tone. Then her real voice hardened. "But *I* could."

Keegan rose to his feet, his fists clenched at his sides. "You're nothing but a stupid thief!"

"Shut up! Shut up, you little fool." Valerie leveled the gun at Keegan, and Beth grabbed Keegan's arm, trying to pull him behind her, but he resisted her efforts.

"Keegan," she warned in a low voice. "Take it easy." She glanced up at Valerie. Part of Clint's theory was right on the mark, it seemed. "You lured me to Big Bear that night, and then you, what? Planted evidence in the car to make the police think that I was Rose?" Beth's headache was subsiding now, and through the panic and fear, her own anger was stirring to life. Because of this woman, her past had been stolen, her memories taken. For two years she'd lived in limbo, in dread of what she might have done, because this woman had tried to take everything from her, including her life. And she'd very nearly succeeded. "But something went wrong, didn't it? I didn't die in that accident. That was a loose end you hadn't counted on."

Valerie's hand was shaking badly now. Beth had gotten to her. "No one should have been able to survive that crash. I did everything right," she all but shouted. "You were the one who messed everything up!"

Completely unhinged now, she lunged toward

them, and Beth's hand closed instinctively over a piece of lumber on the ground. She slammed it against Valerie with all her might.

Stunned, the woman staggered back.

"Run!" Beth screamed at Keegan. "Hurry!"

He dived for cover just as Valerie bellowed like an enraged animal. Blood streaked down her face, but she lurched forward, steadying the gun with both hands. "You're going to pay for that."

Beth rose to her feet and defiantly faced her would-be murderer. She wouldn't go without a fight. If there was anything she knew how to do, it was survive against impossible odds.

Somewhere in the distance a car door slammed, and then another. Valerie heard it, too. She turned her head, listening. Then she swore viciously and spun back to Beth. A split second before she could pull the trigger, something flew out of the darkness and smashed into her.

Clint!

The gun went flying from her hand. As Valerie hit the ground, she, Beth and Clint all scrambled toward the weapon. In the distance, more car doors slammed. Voices rose in the darkness.

Sobbing in desperation, Valerie struggled to her feet and rushed toward the sawdust mounds.

Clint started after her, but just then Keegan came running out of the darkness and launched himself at his father. "Dad! Oh, man, did you ever come in the nick of time!"

Clint grabbed his son and held on tight. His gaze met Beth's in the darkness. "Are you all right? Are either of you hurt?"

"We're okay, Dad." Keegan pulled back and brushed a lock of hair from his eyes. "But that freak is getting away."

"We'll let the cops handle the freak," Clint said as the old abandoned sawmill suddenly came alive with police officers.

"Dad, you should have seen Beth. She was awesome! She so saved my life." Keegan turned to Beth. "That was way cool, the way you kept her talking."

Beth tried to swallow past the lump that had risen in her throat. "Yeah, well, your dad saved us both, I think." She glanced at Clint. "How did you know where to find us?"

"Long story. I'll tell you all about it later." His eyes glimmered in the darkness, making Beth yearn to be in his arms like Keegan. But she didn't want to intrude.

And then a shout came from one of the officers. "She's up there!"

A spotlight was angled to the top of one of the mounds, and for a moment, Valerie was caught in the beam. She turned to stare down at them, and then, as if in slow motion, she began to sink. Her arms flailed for a moment before she completely disappeared.

"Cave-in!" one of the officers shouted.

"Stay away from those mounds until we get some rope to get her out," another one barked. He disengaged himself from the crowd and moved toward Beth, Clint and Keegan. As he drew closer, Beth saw that it was the sheriff she'd seen the day before in the diner. He gave them all a quick once-over. "Everybody okay over here?"

"We're fine," Clint told him. "Glad you got here as soon as you did."

"Your sister said it was a matter of life and death. Guess she wasn't lying." He turned his gaze on Beth. "I'll need statements from all of you, so just stay put for the time being."

"Can't the statements wait until morning?" Clint said with a frown. "These two have been through a pretty terrifying ordeal. I'd like to get them back to the motel."

Beth put a hand on Clint's sleeve. "No, it's okay. I want to get this over with. I'd like to put it behind me, once and for all."

BUT ONCE AND FOR ALL wasn't going to come quite yet. Clint and Beth learned the same night that Valerie had survived the fall. She'd been rushed to the hospital where she remained in stable condition. Charges would soon be filed against her, which meant there would be a trial and reporters to deal with. The nightmare Beth and Keegan had been through wasn't going to be over anytime soon.

Clint had already been down to the police station to get the latest developments when he and Keegan knocked on Beth's door the next morning. As she let them in, her gaze went anxiously to Keegan. She knew it was too soon to tell if he was suffering any aftereffects of the trauma, but at least his easy smile seemed like the old Keegan.

"I don't get it," he said after they'd all talked for a few minutes about their travel plans. Beth had decided not to return immediately to Cooper's Corner, and Keegan was obviously distressed by her decision. "Why can't we all go home together?"

Home. The very word was enough to make Beth tear up. She turned away so neither father nor son could see her emotion.

"How about giving us a few minutes?" Clint said to Keegan.

Keegan glanced from Clint to Beth, then said glumly, "I really messed things up this time, didn't I?"

"You didn't mess anything up," Beth assured him. "I don't think I could have survived last night without you."

That seemed to buoy him for a moment. "Really? You mean it?"

"Of course I mean it. The way you stood up for me..." She glanced at Clint. "You should be very proud of him."

Clint put a hand on Keegan's shoulder. "Oh, I am. I always have been."

Keegan grinned. "I'm going to remember you said that."

"I don't doubt that for a minute," Clint said. "Now scram."

After Keegan left the room, Clint pulled Beth down to sit on the edge of the bed. "I thought you might like to hear the latest on Valerie."

Beth nodded, although she would have been much happier if she never heard the woman's name again. "How's she doing?"

"She'll be okay."

"That's good. I guess." It was hard to feel sympathy for a woman who'd been all too willing to kill a thirteen-year-old boy in order to cover her tracks. Beth might someday be able to forgive Valerie for everything she'd done to her, but she would never forgive her for what she'd done to Keegan.

Beth was finding it hard to forgive herself, as well. If she had never gone to Cooper's Corner, if she hadn't allowed herself to fall for Clint, his son would never have been put in danger.

"Apparently, she's decided to talk," Clint was saying. "I guess she's hoping the prosecution will go easier on her. Between her and Eddie, the sheriff has pretty much pieced together the whole story. They were lovers, it seems. I guess Valerie anticipated there might come a time when she'd need a friend in this town, and Eddie was easy for her to manipulate. The day you checked in, he called and told her that someone was in town asking questions about her. She figured out pretty quickly from his description that it was you. She convinced him and his nephew, Del Ray, to help her get rid of you, but I don't think Del Ray knew what he was getting into. He just thought he could make some quick money by driving your car to Austin and leaving it at the airport. At least that's his story."

"So why did she do it?" Beth asked. "I guess I understand why she wanted to get rid of me, but why did she kill Rose?"

Anger flickered in Clint's eyes. "Because she did to Rose exactly what she did to you. She stole her music."

Beth glanced at him in surprise. "Then Rose wasn't lying about that?"

Clint shook his head. "Apparently not. But she really did have something of an obsession with Valerie. She started out writing her fan letters, and then she began hanging out in front of Valerie's house. The police chased her away on several occasions, but she always came back. Then she started mailing Valerie tapes of her music. Valerie claims she threw them all away at first, but then she developed some kind of writer's block. She couldn't write anymore. Couldn't compose. She said it was like the music had just dried up inside her." Clint's features tightened. "A bit dramatic, if you ask me, but that's her story."

"So she took Rose's songs and claimed they were hers?" Beth asked incredulously.

"When her agent heard them, he told her they were the best songs she'd written in years. I'm sure that must have stung," Clint said dryly.

"I can imagine." Beth shook her head. It was an incredible story. If she hadn't been a part of it, if she hadn't seen firsthand what Valerie Lake was capable of, she probably wouldn't have believed it.

"Anyway," Clint said, "when the first song was recorded and released, Rose started making all these allegations that Valerie had stolen it from her. It was true, of course, but everyone thought she was just some nutcase. But Valerie was afraid that sooner or later, someone might believe Rose. So she got rid of her."

Beth shivered. "As easy as that. And then she stole my song and she wanted to kill me, too. She'd done it once, so why not again, right? But what I don't understand is why she cooked up such an elaborate charade to get rid of me. Why did she claim Rose was stalking her again?"

Clint shrugged. "Because she needed a reason to get rid of her entire staff. By making it look as if Rose had broken into her house and tried to kill her, she was able to convince the police that someone who worked for her must have been in cahoots with Rose. How else could Rose have gotten past the security system?"

"So, not knowing who Rose's accomplice was, she got rid of everyone close to her, and no one was suspicious of her motives."

"Exactly. And since your parents were dead and you had no other family—" He broke off, his gaze faltering. "God, I'm sorry, Beth. I shouldn't have just blurted it out like that."

She smiled sadly. "It's okay. It's not like...I remember them or anything."

"Still—"

She put her hand in his. "It's okay, Clint. Really. I want to hear the rest."

He gazed at her for a long moment, then nodded and gently squeezed her hand. "Once she isolated you from the people you worked with, there was no one to miss you when you disappeared."

In spite of Beth's protestations to the contrary, his words troubled her. There'd been no one in her life to miss her? No one to come looking for her? No one at all?

Tears stung her eyes and she turned away. This was crazy, she told herself. How could she feel a loss for something she'd never had? By all indications, Annie Lockhart had been a loner. Why did that bother Beth so much? Why did that make *her* feel so unbearably lonely?

"Beth," Clint said softly. "Are you sure you want me to go on?"

She drew a breath. "Yes. I have to know what happened. I want to know."

He nodded, but he still didn't look too certain. "Valerie lured you to Big Bear that night. We had that part right. She called and told you she desperately needed your help. She was afraid Rose had found her again, and she needed your assistance to get away. You were the only one she trusted, and you came without hesitation. Evidently, that's the kind of person you were. And still are."

Their gazes met, and Beth felt a little piece of the loneliness start to melt away. "So she tried to kill me by forcing my car over the side of the mountain."

"Yes. She arranged for you to drive a rental car that she'd leased under Rose's name. And she planted Rose's ID in your car, and tossed the briefcase of money and the gun on the mountain where she knew it would be found. She was certain when your body was discovered the police would assume you were Rose Campbell."

"She made such elaborate plans." Beth was almost in awe at the woman's cunning. "She thought of everything. So how could she just disappear without making sure I was dead?"

"She thought she had made sure," Clint said grimly. "She beat the ambulance to the hospital that night, and hung out in the E.R. until they brought you in. She heard one of the paramedics say you'd gone into cardiac arrest. You were clinically dead. And then sometime later, one of the doctors who'd been working on you came out of the operating room and

screamed at one of the nurses. Valerie overheard another nurse tell her not to take it personally, because
Dr. Berger was always impossible to deal with after
he'd lost a patient. Valerie assumed that patient was
you. She left the hospital, certain you were dead. Of
course, what she didn't count on was your amazing
strength. I don't know of anyone else who could have
survived what you've been through, Beth. I admire
you. I want you to know that. And I'll always be
grateful to you for saving Keegan's life.''

A lump rose in Beth's throat. "You make it sound
like this is goodbye."

His own eyes misted. "I guess I'm afraid it is."
He glanced down at their linked hands. "You're not
coming back to Cooper's Corner, are you?"

She shook her head. "I...can't. Not yet. Annie
Lockhart had a life in California. Valerie said that my
parents were dead, but there must be someone out
there who cared about me. I have to find out for sure.
I have to find out who Annie Lockhart was. Please
try to understand, Clint."

"I do understand." He lifted her hand to his lips.
"But I want you to understand something, too. No
matter what you find out about Annie Lockhart, you'll
always be Beth to me."

CHAPTER FIFTEEN

THE HOUSE WHERE Annie Lockhart grew up was a modest, Spanish-style cottage nestled among palm trees, hibiscus bushes and brilliant splashes of bougainvillea. Beth stood on the sunny walkway in front of the house, gazing at the stucco facade for several long minutes as she waited for the memories to bombard her.

None did.

The house stirred nothing inside her, but she knew it was the right one. In the few days that she'd been in Los Angeles, she'd done her research well. She'd lived in this house until her mother died when Beth—Annie—was twenty-five. She'd stayed on for three more years before she'd sold the house, and had, at the same time, quit her teaching job at a private school a few miles away. That was when she'd gone to work for Valerie Lake.

There had to be so many memories locked inside that house, Beth thought sadly. And yet she couldn't remember a single one of them.

"Annie? Is that really you?"

It took Beth a moment to realize the woman next door was calling to her. She stood on her front porch, one hand shading her eyes as she gazed at Beth. "You are Annie Lockhart, aren't you?"

"Yes." As she slowly approached the woman, Beth could see that she was perhaps in her late fifties and attractive, with curly blond hair and vivid blue eyes that danced excitedly as she waited for Beth.

"Oh, my heavens," she said dramatically, putting a hand to her heart. "It really *is* you!"

She flew down the front steps and smothered Beth in an overwhelming embrace. The woman was slight, but she was strong. "Let me look at you!" She held Beth at arm's length, and her eyes welled with tears. "I'd forgotten how much you look like Nancy."

"Nancy?"

"Why, your mother, of course." The woman's gaze clouded suddenly. "I'm Connie Johnson. You don't remember me, do you?"

"I'm sorry," Beth said helplessly. "I don't remember anything. I was in an accident—"

Connie nodded. "I know. I read all about it in the paper. Someone tried to kill you—that awful woman you went to work for. I couldn't believe it when I saw your picture in the paper. And then I read the article, and sure enough, it mentioned your name." She shook her head, gazing up at Beth with motherly concern. "You've been through so much, what with your mother dying so suddenly, and…everything else." She took Beth's arm. "Come inside," she urged. "Let me fix you something to drink and we can talk. I'll tell you all about your mom. You'd like that, wouldn't you? She was my best friend, you know.…"

They talked and talked. Connie was a veritable fount of information, and Beth couldn't get enough.

"I was so surprised when you gave up teaching,"

Connie said. "You always loved it so. But after Nancy died, everything seemed to change for you. It was as if...I don't know...you were searching for something."

Beth thought instantly of Clint. He'd been on her mind constantly since she'd arrived in L.A. She wanted to call him so badly she couldn't stand it, but they'd agreed that day at the motel that she needed some space, needed some time to reacquaint herself with her old life. With Annie's life.

And so here she was. Without Clint. Without Keegan. Beth didn't think she'd ever been so lonely in her life. So...lost.

"You're very much like your mother, you know," Connie said softly. "And I don't mean just in appearance. You have her same gentle qualities, her sweet smile. You always did."

Beth smiled. "I wish I could remember her."

"You will in time." Connie patted her hand. "But for now, maybe I can help you." She left the room for a few minutes, and when she returned, she carried several thick photo albums with her. "I know there are bound to be snapshots of your mother in some of these. And of you, too, Annie. We were all very close." She began flipping through the pages. "I'm sorry to say I don't have any photos of your father, though. He died when you were very young, before you and Nancy moved next door. Ah, here we are."

She handed Beth the photo album, and Beth glanced down. A woman with long dark hair and violet-blue eyes smiled up at her. It might have been a picture of Beth, except that she knew it wasn't. It was her mother.

Her mother...

Beth's eyes filled with tears. She didn't remember the woman, and yet she did. She had no specific memory of her, and yet she could almost feel the warmth of her smile, her love.

Beth traced the outline of her mother's face with her fingertip. She'd been so beautiful, so kind and gentle, and she'd loved her daughter with all her heart. Somehow Beth knew that. What a devastating loss it must have been when her mother died. For a moment, Beth's heart knotted with pain.

"I don't remember her," she said softly. "Not really. I can't remember the places we went together or the things we did, but somehow I know her. Somehow I can feel her still with me." She looked up with a wistful smile. "Does that make sense?"

Connie's own eyes were brimming with tears. "It makes perfect sense. She did love you, Annie. She loved you more than anything in this world. I know she's been with you all this time, watching over you. She's been your guardian angel."

Beth thought about what the doctors had told her in the hospital. It was a miracle she'd survived that car crash. Had her mother had a hand in her survival? Beth wasn't a particularly spiritual person, or at least she'd never regarded herself as one, but it comforted her now to think that her mother had been with her on that mountain.

She turned the page of the photo album and saw a picture of herself. She was younger, and the white streak was missing from her hair, but other than that, Beth didn't think she'd changed all that much.

A young man stood beside her in the photo, and

they had their arms wrapped around each other. He was smiling. Beth wasn't. "Who is that?" she asked curiously.

Connie leaned over to have a look. "Oh." She drew back. "That's Rick."

"Rick?"

Connie glanced away. "Rick Braiden. Your fiancé."

"DAD, WHEN IS BETH coming back?" Keegan queried one night after dinner. They'd been home a week, and Clint was relieved that his son seemed to be suffering no aftershocks from the close call he'd had. If anything, he relished the new stature he'd acquired in his friends' eyes. He was no longer just a boy with a troubled past. He was a kid who'd almost been murdered by a psychopath. If he played it just right, his new reputation would serve him in good stead for years to come.

"Did you hear me?" he asked impatiently. "When is Beth coming back?"

"I don't know," Clint said truthfully. In fact, he didn't know if she was ever coming back. He hadn't heard a word from her since they'd parted at the motel, and he didn't know how to reach her. She'd completely cut herself off, and the knowledge that the lack of communication had been his idea didn't make him feel a damn bit better. He'd thought she needed the time and space to come to terms with her past without the present—without him—confusing the issue. But now Clint realized how stupid he'd been to let her go out to L.A. alone. He should have gone with her. He should have made sure she came back.

And just how would you do that if she didn't want to? a little voice taunted him. *Drag her back by the hair of her head? Face it, you're not the caveman type.*

Maybe he hadn't been in the past, Clint thought grimly, but desperate times called for desperate measures. And he was getting pretty damn desperate to see Beth.

"Why don't we just go out there and get her?" Keegan's question echoed Clint's thoughts so precisely it was almost scary.

"Because we've got to give her some time to find out about her old life," Clint explained halfheartedly.

"Why does she need to know about her old life?" Keegan wondered. "She's got a perfectly good life right here in Cooper's Corner."

Clint smiled. "You like it here, don't you, Son?"

"Well, yeah. It's home. It's Beth's home, too." He paused. "Look, Dad, I really think you should go out there and get her."

"It's not that easy—"

"Sure it is," Keegan said stubbornly. "I've been thinking. What if she gets out there in L.A. and finds out she has, you know, a boyfriend or something? Or even a husband? What would you do then?"

I'd be miserable, Clint thought. And furious as hell that he'd let Beth slip from his grasp.

A boyfriend? A husband? No. He wouldn't let himself consider the possibility.

But what if there was someone else in her life? What if she was with him at that very moment?

Clint almost groaned in frustration.

"So are you going out there or what?" Keegan demanded.

"No, I'm not," Clint said firmly. Not at this very moment, anyway. But after another night spent tossing and turning, he might just feel differently.

BETH HAD NO IDEA whether or not she'd be able to recognize Rick Braiden from his picture, but as she glanced around the elegant restaurant, a man rose from a table near the window and waved.

For a moment, the urge to glance behind her, to make sure she was the woman he was waving to, was almost irresistible. But then Beth saw the same blond hair and hazel eyes from his picture, and she reluctantly started toward him.

He smiled as she approached the table, and came around to hold out her chair for her. Once they were settled, his gaze locked with hers. "I can't believe I'm actually sitting across a table from you. It's been a long time."

Something flickered in his eyes as his gaze swept over her. "You look amazing. I like what you've done to your hair."

She smiled. "What nature did to my hair, you mean. It grew back that way after the accident."

His expression sobered. "I can't believe you almost died and I didn't even know about it. When I heard your voice on the phone this morning—" He broke off, reaching for her hand. "Amnesia," he said softly. "It's hard to imagine. But you really don't remember me, do you?"

"I'm sorry." She wanted to withdraw her hand from his, but somehow Beth thought it would be impolite. After all, they'd once been engaged, according to Connie Johnson. And according to Rick, too, when she'd phoned that morning.

"I hope you don't mind that I called you," she said. "I just found out yesterday that we were once...close."

He smiled and squeezed her hand. "We were very close."

Oh, God, could this be any more awkward? she thought. "I guess I just needed to see if I would remember anything when I saw you again. If I would feel anything..." She trailed off, embarrassed.

"And do you?"

He was gazing at her so intently, Beth wondered now what had possessed her to call him. She hadn't meant to give him the wrong idea. She'd just needed to see him, for her own peace of mind, but maybe that had been selfish on her part.

"I'm sorry," she said again. "Maybe I shouldn't have called."

"I'm glad you did. There're some things I've wanted to say to you for a very long time, Annie. Now is as good a time as any, I guess." His voice had changed, hardened.

Beth's heart quickened uneasily. "What is it?"

"Since you don't remember me, I assume you also don't remember what happened between us. Why we broke up."

She shook her head, a premonition of something unpleasant settling over her.

"You dumped me," he said bluntly. "You started pulling away after your mother died. We were supposed to have been married the next month, but you

put it off because of your grief. Perfectly understandable, of course. Except that you kept putting it off.
Until the next month, until the next year. I never
could pin you down on a date. We had it out one
night and you finally told me that you had put your
house up for sale, you'd quit your teaching job and
you were starting a whole new career—a new life—
without me."

"I'm...sorry," Beth said again, realizing she
sounded like a broken record. But what else was there
to say? Rick seemed like a nice enough man, and
she'd treated him badly, by the sounds of it. But she
couldn't change the past. She didn't even remember
it.

"You know, I think I hated you there for a while,"
he said. "I was bitter and resentful, and I wanted to
hurt you the way you'd hurt me. I figured if you were
starting a new life, I could do the same, right? I'd
show you. The very next day after we broke up, I
accepted a transfer to New York. It only took me
about six months in the Big Apple to realize that
you'd done me the biggest favor of my life. You'd
faced something that I wasn't ready to face."

"And that was?" she asked reluctantly.

"We'd outgrown each other, Annie. We'd known
each other since we were in high school. We loved
each other, but we were no longer in love. Maybe we
never were," he said a bit sadly. "Anyway, when I
finally realized you'd done the right thing, I started
looking at life very differently. And I met someone."
He grinned. "Someone special."

"I'm glad for you," Beth murmured. The man sit-

ting across from her meant nothing to her now, but
he had once. She wished him only the best.

"I'm married," he said, holding up his left hand.
"We're expecting our first child in a couple of
months."

"That's great." Beth felt a pang of something she
didn't want to name. She thought of Clint and Keegan, and her heart ached with loneliness. What was
she doing here, anyway? Why wasn't she back home
in Cooper's Corner with the man of her dreams and
his son, whom she adored? Hadn't she learned
enough about Annie's life? Wasn't it time to get back
to Beth's?

"I hope you don't take this the wrong way, but the
day you dumped me turned out to be the best day of
my life," Rick said ironically. "And you know
what?" He leaned across the table, his amber gaze
suddenly misty. "Even though you don't remember
me, I'll always care about you, Annie. And I hope
you find what I've found."

"Maybe I already have," she said softly.

He sat back in his chair and smiled. "Then why
are you wasting your time with me?"

IT WAS NOT QUITE TIME to go back to Cooper's Corner. Beth had one more stop to make. One more person she had to visit.

And there was still something she hadn't been able
to resolve in her own mind. She loved Clint and Keegan. Loved them with all her heart. She knew that
now, knew it without a doubt. But she didn't have
her memory back. There were large chunks of her
past that remained a mystery to her.

It was easy to go back to being Beth when Annie Lockhart's life meant nothing to her. But...what if someday it all came back to her? What if someday she woke up and saw Annie in the mirror instead of Beth?

What would happen to her and Clint then? Would he still love her? Would she still love him? And could she ask him to take such a risk?

All those doubts churned inside Beth as she followed Connie Johnson's directions to the cemetery. Once she was there, it took her only a few moments to locate her parents' graves. She'd brought flowers for both of them, and when she'd arranged the blooms to her satisfaction in the urn vases, Beth sat down on the grass between the two graves.

Her father had died when she was young, Connie had told her. Maybe that was why Beth didn't feel the same pull, the same ethereal connection to him that she did with her mother. Or maybe mothers and daughters were always closer. Beth didn't know. She just knew that it was her mother's voice she desperately needed to hear at that moment.

She took out the picture Connie had given her and placed it near her mother's grave. Her mother smiled up at her, and Beth closed her eyes.

"I miss you so much," she whispered. "I know I don't remember you, but I know I loved you, and I know you loved me. I can still feel that love."

A breeze whispered through her hair like a caress.

"I've met a man," she said. "A wonderful man. He has a thirteen-year-old son. I adore them both, but I'm afraid to love them. I'm afraid I'll end up hurting them." She drew a tremulous breath. "What if I get

my memory back someday, and I decide I'd rather be
Annie than Beth? What if I discover...I don't love
them?''

Is that really why you're so afraid? a voice inside
her asked. Beth could almost believe it was her
mother's voice. *Are you afraid of hurting them...or
are you afraid of being hurt?*

"What do you mean?"

*Clint fell in love with Beth, not Annie. Isn't that
what frightens you so much?*

"I don't know," she admitted. "But I know I don't
want to hurt them."

*Love never comes with guarantees. Besides, you
and Annie aren't so different. If he loves you, he could
fall in love with her. And if he's the man you say he
is, I think Annie could fall in love with him, too. He
sounds like the man of her dreams.*

"He's the man of any woman's dreams," Beth said
with a smile. "He's the kind of man I could fall in
love with every day of my life."

*Then I think you have your answer. It's time to go
home...Beth.*

BETH HAD BEEN GONE for two weeks. God, it seemed
like an eternity. Sometimes the loneliness was almost
unbearable, but Clint was a survivor, just like Beth.
They'd both get through this somehow, apart or together, and somehow they'd get on with their lives.
One thing Clint knew for sure—he'd never shut his
son out of his life again. Keegan was everything to
him.

We'll be all right, Clint told himself sternly. He
just needed some time, that was all. Early evening,

when the piano in the gathering room remained silent, was the hardest part of the day. That was when it seemed as if the hole in his heart might never heal.

"Clint?"

He looked up. Maureen was standing in the doorway, her brows drawn together in worry. "What is it?" he said sharply. "Is it Keegan?"

"No, Keegan's fine. I just saw him out back with the twins."

Not Beth, Clint silently prayed. *Please, not Beth.*

"It's Dan D'Angelo," Maureen said, dropping down in the chair across from the desk. "He's dead."

Clint stared at her in shock. Her ex-partner was dead? "How? When?"

"They found his body this morning on a golf course down in Florida. They're saying it was some kind of freak accident, but I don't believe it. Neither does Quigg."

"Nevil?" The very name made Clint's blood boil. The thought of that animal still out there somewhere, still a threat to Maureen and the girls… "What are you going to do?"

She shrugged. "What can I do? I have to live my life." She shook her head. "Poor Dan. He was a good partner."

"He was a good man," Clint agreed. They fell silent, both lost in gloomy thoughts, until gradually Clint became aware of a distant sound, a hauntingly familiar, impossibly beautiful sound.

"Is it just me," he said into the silence, "or do you hear music?"

Maureen turned her head toward the doorway, listening. "That's the piano," she said. "It sounds like Beth."

Clint half rose, then dropped back to his chair. "That's impossible."

"Why is it impossible?" When he didn't answer, she said, "For goodness' sakes, go see. I know you're dying to."

They both stood, and Clint strode around the desk. At the door, he came back and took Maureen's arms. "Everything's going to be okay, you know. I'm not going to let anything happen to you and the girls."

She smiled. "Always the big brother, aren't you?"

"I guess I can't help it." He kissed her lightly on the forehead.

"Go," she said. "You're getting way too mushy in your old age."

"Yeah," he said, a little surprised. "Kind of scary, isn't it?"

BETH KNEW THE MOMENT Clint entered the room. She had her back to him and she didn't turn, but it didn't matter. She knew his footfall. She knew his scent. She knew the very essence of him.

Her fingers faltered on the keys and she did turn then. He was there behind her, so close she could reach out and touch him. She resisted the temptation and merely stared up at him.

"Hello, Clint."

"When did you get back? Or are you back?" He looked doubtful all of a sudden. "Is this just a quick visit?"

She started to say something, then saw all the curious faces behind them and said softly, "Could we take a walk?"

A frown flittered across his brow, but he nodded.

They stepped outside. Summer had come in earnest to the Berkshires, and the gardens were bursting with color and fragrance. They walked silently down the long driveway, lined on either side with oak trees planted in pairs every time a set of twins was born in the Cooper family. The youngest trees had been planted to honor Randi and Robyn.

The Coopers had a long tradition in this town, Beth thought. They could trace their ancestors back for generations. Beth Young's life had begun two years ago, when she'd awakened from a coma.

"So did you find what you were looking for in California?" Clint finally asked her.

"I think so. I located a friend or two. They seemed like nice people. They told me I'd been a nice person. But what else were they going to say, right?" She smiled. "I was born and raised in Los Angeles. My father died when I was five. My mother and I were very close. I lived at home all through college. I graduated from UCLA with a music degree and I was a teacher for years. When my mother died suddenly, I quit teaching. I don't know why. I guess I needed a change. That's when I went to work for Valerie."

"These friends you spoke of." He seemed to be choosing his words carefully. "Was there anyone special?"

She nodded. "Yes. I had a fiancé. We broke up just before I went to work for Valerie. He said I dumped him, and that it was the best thing that ever happened to him." Her laugh was rueful.

Clint wasn't amused. "You saw him then?"

Something in his voice made her gaze up at him. "Yes, I saw him. He seemed like a nice guy. They were all nice. I had a nice life." She stopped walking. "Annie Lockhart had a nice life, but it wasn't my life, Clint. My life is here, in Cooper's Corner. I couldn't wait to get back."

His gaze held hers in the fading light. "You didn't call," he said with the slightest hint of accusation.

"Because we agreed not to. And I think it was for the best. I really do. It was important that I give that life—Annie's life—a chance. Do you understand?"

He shrugged. "Sure." But he still didn't sound convinced.

"I've been so afraid of hurting you and Keegan, and of hurting myself, that I've tried to hold back my feelings. Tried to protect us all. I keep asking myself what would happen if I wake up one day and my memory has returned. What if I'm no longer Beth Young, but Annie Lockhart? I keep wondering what would happen...to us."

"And did you come up with any answers?"

She turned away. It was hard to concentrate when he was gazing at her so intently. "I think we'd just have to fall in love all over again," she said softly.

She heard the sharp intake of his breath, and she turned at last to face him. "I love you, Clint. I don't know if I'll ever get my memory back, not completely. So I don't know what tomorrow will bring. All I know is that I love you and Keegan more than life itself, and I don't want to live without you."

He was silent for so long that Beth started to wonder if he was having second thoughts. If he'd discovered, while she was away, that he didn't love her, after all.

Then something glittered in his eyes. Something warm and familiar. "You could really fall in love with me all over again?"

"I fall in love with you every time I see you," she said. "You haven't noticed?"

"It's hard to see," he said gruffly, "with all these stars in my eyes."

They were standing on a hillock that overlooked the lush, dreamy valley. Dusk had fallen, and lights were beginning to flicker on in the village. The last rays of a spectacular sunset backlit the distant mountains. It was a beautiful place, a beautiful scene, but Clint still hadn't told Beth what she wanted to hear.

She drew a deep breath. "I don't think I've ever been out here before."

"I've always thought this would be the perfect spot for a house," Clint said. "A rambling farmhouse with a long porch where we could watch sunsets in the summer."

Something quickened inside her. *We?*

He took a few steps away from her. "I thought Keegan's bedroom could go over here, on the second floor, so he'd be up in the trees. He'd like that." Clint walked back toward her. "And your piano could go here."

Beth's heart was beating so hard by now that she thought it would surely burst. "My piano?"

"In a big bay window, so you can look out at the mountains and the valley while you play. And maybe you might even watch for me to come home in the evenings."

She put a hand to her mouth. He was getting closer. So close to uttering what she desperately wanted to hear.

"What do you think, Beth?" He gazed down at her. His eyes were shimmering in the twilight. "Do you think you could be happy in a house like that?"

She blinked back tears and nodded. "If you and Keegan were here, I don't think I could be happy anywhere else."

"Good," he said, wrapping his arms around her and holding her close. "Because I love you, and I don't intend to ever let you go. I don't care what your name is."

She laughed, and then she cried, and as Clint bent to kiss her, a stray breeze touched a set of wind chimes he'd hung high in the trees.

The soft, sweet sound echoed the music that flowed so freely from Beth's heart.

Welcome to Twin Oaks—
the new B and B in Cooper's Corner,
Massachusetts. Bed-and-breakfast
will never be the same!
COOPER'S CORNER
a Harlequin continuity series
continues with
FAR FROM OVER
by Bobby Hutchinson

Chance Maguire was reeling from the news. He'd just been informed he was the father of three-year-old twin girls...and they'd been kidnapped! Chance hadn't even known his ex-wife, Maureen Cooper, had been pregnant when they divorced. He was outraged, angry and confused. But concern for the daughters he'd never met had Chance rushing to Twin Oaks, Maureen's B and B.

Here's a preview!

CHAPTER ONE

MAUREEN GLANCED at the clock on the kitchen wall and shuddered. The twins had been gone three hours and ten minutes. She was afraid to leave the house in case Nevil called again, but being here was making her crazy.

She wanted to be alone, to think, to plan, but there was a steady stream of people coming and going. They came and left again, shocked and wanting to help.

She should have gone into the small office, where she'd be alone, but some rational part of her just couldn't be rude to those who came to offer sympathy and assistance. So she sat at the kitchen table, unable to do anything except make and discard frantic, unrealistic plans for getting the twins back safe and sound.

She heard the front doorbell ring but ignored it. There were enough other people around to answer it. It would undoubtedly be more neighbors bringing food and assuring her they hadn't told a soul.

She was dimly aware of Keegan's voice, greeting Dr. Dorn. There was a rumble of low male voices, but she paid no attention.

"Hello, Reen."

Her back was to the doorway, and she froze, not looking around.

Only one man had ever called her Reen. She turned slowly, thinking she was hallucinating. For a long moment she was speechless, and then his name came out, no more than a whisper.

"Chance?" She stared up at him, wondering as she had several times these past few hours if this could, after all, be just a horrible nightmare. What other explanation could there be for his appearance here in her kitchen?

For one mindless moment, all she wanted to do was throw herself into his strong, capable arms, but then painful memories intervened. He wasn't her husband or her lover anymore. He was a stranger, a cold-hearted, remote stranger who'd rejected her at a time in her life when she'd most needed him.

"What are you doing here, Chance?"

She could see that he was angry.

"I think we have some talking to do, Reen."

There had been at least seven others in the kitchen, but now, just when Maureen would have welcomed their presence, everyone melted away and she and Chance were suddenly alone.

He sat down at the table, and Maureen stared across at him. It had been nearly five years since she'd last laid eyes on him.

He was older, but the charisma that had attracted her the very first time she'd met him was as strong as ever. Chance gave off sexual energy the way other men wore aftershave.

"What—what are you doing here, Chance? How

did you find out—'' Her throat closed up and she had to swallow hard.

"About my children? Keegan called me.''

Maureen felt amazed and resentful that her nephew would take it upon himself to call Chance.

"He had no right to do that.''

"He didn't do it all on his own, Reen. It was the doctor's suggestion. But regardless of who thought of it, I'm very glad it happened. Now, I think it's time for you to tell me exactly what's happened to *our* daughters.''

He was furious with her. She knew the signs, knew them all too well from having lived with him for the fourteen months their marriage had lasted.

His lack of visible emotion had always driven her in the opposite direction. She'd responded to his controlled anger with loud sarcasm, hollering, once even throwing a hardcover book at him in utter, absolute frustration.

Right now she had no energy to spare for such histrionics. She drew in a shaky breath and, as if she was reading from a police report, gave him the bare details of the kidnapping.

He shook his head, frowning, and impatience was evident in his tone. "I don't understand. This is obviously a quiet, backwoods little town. Who the hell would do a thing like this, and why?''